KT-547-803

The Peculiar Life of a Lonely Postman

SWANSEA LIBRARIES

6000223802

Published by Hesperus Nova
Hesperus Press Limited
28 Mortimer Street, London W1W 7RD
www.hesperuspress.com

First published by Hesperus Press Limited, 2014
First published in French edition © 2005, *Facteur émotif* / XYZ éditeur

This edition © 2014, Hesperus Press, through Allied Authors Agency, Belgium.

English Translation © Liedewy Hawke, 2008

Typeset by Sarah Newitt
Printed in Great Britain by CPI Group (UK) Ltd, Croydon, CR0 4YY

ISBN: 978-1-84391-536-2

All rights reserved. This book is sold subject to the condition that it shall
not be resold, lent, hired out or otherwise circulated without the express
prior consent of the publisher.

The Peculiar Life
of a Lonely Postman

Denis Thériault

Translated by Liedewy Hawke

To Louise and Guy

Swirling like water
against rugged rocks,
time goes around and around

Beech Street, rue des Hêtres, was for the most part lined with maples. Glancing down the road, one saw a double row of four- or five-storey apartment buildings, with outside staircases providing access to the upper floors. The street had 115 of those staircases, which added up to 1,495 steps. Bilodo knew this because he had counted and re-counted them, since he climbed every one of those stairs every single morning. These 1,495 steps, each with an average height of 20 centimetres, made for a total of 299 metres. More than one and a half times the height of Place Ville-Marie. He in fact hoofed it up the equivalent of the Eiffel Tower day after day, rain or shine, not to mention the fact that he had to go back down, too. Bilodo did not view this vertical marathon as an achievement. It was a daily challenge rather; without it, his life would have seemed quite flat to him. Considering himself a kind of athlete, he felt a particular kinship with long-distance hikers, those bold trekking specialists, and felt the odd twinge of regret that, among all the admirable forms of endurance sports, there wasn't a category for stair climbers. He would almost certainly have put up a good show in the 1,500 steps or 250-metre ascent–descent. If at the Olympic Games there had been a stair-scaling event, Bilodo would have stood an excellent chance of qualifying, perhaps even of mounting the ultimate, glorious top step of the podium.

In the meantime, he was a postman.

He was twenty-seven years old.

* * *

Bilodo had been tracing the same postal route in Saint-Janvier-des-Âmes for five years now. He had actually moved into the heart of this working-class district so as to be closer to his job. During all those years of loyal service, he had missed only one day of work to attend the funeral of his parents, who had died in a funicular accident in Quebec City. He could be described as a steady employee.

In the morning, at the Depot, he began by sorting his post for the day. He had to arrange all the envelopes and parcels into the order they were to be delivered and tie them into bundles, which a postal employee in a van would transport to secure boxes along the route. Bilodo managed to carry out this tedious task with exceptional speed. He had his own sorting method, which was inspired by both the card-dealing technique of croupiers and the expertise of knife-throwers: like blades flung with lethal accuracy, the envelopes would leave his hand, fly towards the target, and slip into the appropriate pigeonhole. He rarely missed. This remarkable skill allowed him to finish well before the others – a good thing, too, because he could then escape. Bilodo couldn't think of anything more exciting than taking off, decamping, drinking in the fresh air and savouring the fragrance of a new day while walking about in the morning hours without anyone telling him what to do.

It wasn't all roses, of course. There were those blasted advertising flyers to be delivered; the backaches, the sprains and other run-of-the-mill injuries; there were the crushing summer heatwaves, the autumn rains that left you soaked to the skin, the black ice in winter, which turned the city into a perilous ice palace, and the cold that could be biting, just like the dogs for that matter – a postman's natural enemies. But the moral satisfaction of knowing oneself to be indispensable to the community made up for these drawbacks. Bilodo felt he took part in the life of the neighbourhood, that he had a discreet but essential role in it. For him, delivering post was a mission he accomplished conscientiously, knowing he contributed in this way to the maintenance of order in the universe. He wouldn't have wanted to swap places with anyone in the world. Except perhaps with another postman.

* * *

Bilodo usually had lunch at the Madelinot, a restaurant located not far from the Depot, and, after his dessert, he'd spend a bit of time doing calligraphy, that art of fine penmanship, which he practised as an amateur. Getting out his exercise book and nibs, he would settle himself at the counter and transcribe a few words from a newspaper or an item from the menu. He'd grow absorbed in the choreographic movements of the nib on the paper, waltz among the downstrokes and upstrokes of Italian hand, perform volts with opulent uncial or cross swords with Gothic script, fancying himself as one of those worthy medieval copyist monks who lived on ink alone, ruining their eyes, their fingers freezing but their soul aglow.

Bilodo's colleagues at the Depot were baffled. As they flocked noisily into the Madelinot at lunchtime, they jeered at his calligraphic efforts, calling them scribbles. Bilodo didn't take offence, because they were his friends, and all they were really guilty of was ignorance. Unless one was an informed and devoted enthusiast like himself, how could one possibly savour the subtle beauty of a pen stroke, the delicately balanced proportions of a well-executed line? The only person who seemed capable of appreciating these things was Tania, the waitress. She was always pleasant and appeared genuinely interested in what he was doing and told him she thought it was beautiful. A sensitive young woman, to be sure. Bilodo liked her very much. He always left her a large tip. If he'd been a little more observant, he would have noticed she often watched him from her spot near the till and at dessert time always served him the biggest piece of pie. But he didn't notice. Or did he choose not to?

Bilodo no longer looked at other women since Ségolène had come into his life.

* * *

Bilodo lived on the tenth floor of a high-rise in a one-bedroom apartment decorated with film posters, which he shared with his goldfish, Bill. In the evening he played Halo or Call of Duty, and then ate his dinner, a ready meal, while watching TV. He hardly ever went out. Only the odd Friday, when Robert became too insistent. Robert, a fellow postal worker, was assigned to the clearing of postboxes, and was also his best friend. Robert went out often, almost every night, but Bilodo rarely agreed to come along because he didn't really care for those smoky nightspots, those earsplitting raves, and those clubs with nude dancers his friend dragged him off to. He preferred to stay at home, far from the hustle and bustle of the world and from female posteriors – more so than ever since Ségolène had entered his life.

Anyhow, he had better things to do with his evenings. Bilodo was extremely busy in his apartment at night. After the TV and the dishes, he bolted the door and indulged in his secret vice.

2

Bilodo was an unusual postman.

Among the thousands of soulless pieces of paper he delivered on his rounds, he occasionally came across a personal letter – a less and less common item in this era of email, and all the more fascinating for being so rare. When that happened, Bilodo felt as excited as a prospector spotting a gold nugget in his pan. He did not deliver that letter. Not right away. He took it home and steamed it open. That's what kept him so busy at night in the privacy of his apartment.

Bilodo was an inquisitive postman.

He himself never received personal post. He would've liked to but didn't have anyone to whom he was close enough to correspond. He used to send letters to himself, but the experience had been a disappointment. He'd gradually stopped, and didn't really miss it; he didn't miss himself. More alluring by far were letters from others. Real letters, written by real people who preferred the sensual act of writing by hand, the delightfully languorous anticipation of the reply, to the reptilian coldness of the keyboard and instantaneity of the Internet – people for whom the act of writing was a deliberate choice and in some cases, one sensed, a matter of principle, a stand taken in favour of a lifestyle not quite so determined by the race against time and the obligation to perform.

There were those comical letters Doris T. wrote from Maria in the Gaspé Peninsula to her sister Gwendoline to fill her in on the local gossip, and those heart-rending ones Richard L., detained in the Port Cartier prison, sent to his young son, Hugo. There were those long mystical epistles Sister Régine of the Congrégation du Saint-Rosaire in Rimouski dispatched to her old friend Germaine, and those erotic little tales Laetitia D., a young nurse temporarily exiled in the Yukon, composed for her lonely fiancé, and also those strange missives in which a mysterious O. gave advice to a certain N. on how to safely invoke various supernatural beings. There was anything and everything, coming from here, there, and everywhere: letters from close relatives and faraway correspondents, letters from beer tasters comparing notes, from globetrotters writing to their mothers, from retired steam locomotive firemen listing their bumps and bruises. There were those overly reassuring letters servicemen dispatched from Afghanistan to their anxious wives, and those worried words uncles wrote to their nieces concerning secrets that shouldn't be revealed for anything in the world, and those Dear John or Dear Mary letters in which circus acrobats in Las Vegas broke up with their former lovers, and there were even hate letters crammed with insults spilling out onto the envelope.

But above all there were love letters. Because even after Valentine's Day, love remained the most common denominator, the subject linking the greatest number of pens. Love in every grammatical form and every possible tone, dished up in every imaginable shape: passionate letters or courteous ones, sometimes suggestive and sometimes chaste, either calm or dramatic, occasionally violent, often lyrical, and especially moving when the feelings were expressed in simple terms, and never quite so touching as when the emotions hid between the lines, burning away almost invisibly behind a screen of innocuous words.

Once he'd read and reread the letter of the day, had savoured it down to the very marrow, Bilodo made a photocopy of it for his records. He put this in a folder, the colour of which corresponded to the subject, which he placed in a fireproof filing cabinet. He would slip the original letter back into its envelope, deftly seal it, and drop it into the addressee's letterbox the next day as if nothing had happened. He had been practising this clandestine activity for two years now. It was a crime, he was well aware of that, but guilt paled into insignificance beside supreme curiosity. No one was hurt by it, after all, and he himself didn't risk much as long as he continued to be careful. Who was going to worry that the delivery of a letter was twenty-four hours late? And, for a start, who could know it was late?

* * *

Bilodo intercepted letters from about thirty correspondents in this way. All together they formed a kind of soap opera with multiple plots. Or rather half of a soap opera, whose other half, the one of the 'outgoing post', was unfortunately unavailable to him. But he liked to make up that other part, to draft elaborate replies he never posted, and when another letter arrived he was often amazed to see how naturally it fitted in with his own secret reply.

That's how it was. Bilodo lived vicariously. To the dullness of real life he preferred his infinitely more colourful, more thrilling, interior serial drama. And of all the clandestine letters that constituted this fascinating little virtual world, none mobilized or enchanted him more than the ones from Ségolène.

3

Ségolène lived at Pointe-à-Pitre in Guadeloupe and wrote regularly to a certain Gaston Grandpré, who rented an apartment on rue des Hêtres. Bilodo had been intercepting her letters for two years now, and whenever he spotted one while sorting his post, he always experienced the same shock, the same shiver of awe. He would quietly slip that letter inside his jacket and only allow himself to show any emotion once he was alone on the road, turning the envelope over and over, fingering the exciting promise. He could have opened it right away and revelled in the words it concealed, but he'd rather wait. All he granted himself was the fleeting pleasure of inhaling the fragrance of oranges wafting up from the letter before bravely putting it back in his pocket, and he kept it there all day, against his heart, resisting temptation, drawing out the pleasure until evening, until after the washing up was done. Then the time had come. He would burn a few drops of citrus oil, light a few candles, put on a disc of dreamy Norwegian jazz, and then, at last, he unsealed the envelope, gently reached into its inner fold, and read:

Under clear water
the newborn baby
swims like a playful otter

Bilodo could see it. He vividly saw that stark-naked baby in the aqueous luminescence of the postnatal swimming pool while it swam towards him as if he were its mother, as if it were swimming towards the outstretched arms of a mermaid who would be its mother and who was watching him with deep blue flabbergasted-salamander eyes. It didn't know it couldn't swim, hadn't forgotten how to yet. It had no idea water was dangerous, a foreign element, that it could drown in it. The baby was ignorant of all this, it just moved about, followed its instinct, kept its mouth closed, and simply swam. Bilodo saw that young pinniped clearly – that funny underwater gnome with the crinkly features of infants and nostrils ringed with bubbles, as it glided through the voluptuous water, and Bilodo laughed because it was unexpected, because it was amusing, touching. And *he* thought he was floating too. He could hear the water buzzing against his eardrums. He felt as though he was in that swimming pool together with that baby. For such was the suggestive power of all those strange little poems Ségolène wrote: they made you feel things, made you see them.

The letters from the Guadeloupean woman contained nothing else. Always a single sheet of paper on which was written a single poem. It wasn't much, yet it was generous, since those poems nourished you as much as a whole novel – they were long in your soul, where they echoed forever. Bilodo learned them by heart and recited them to himself on his morning round. He treasured them up in the top drawer of his bedside table and liked spreading them around him at night, constructing a kind of mystical circle, and rereading them one after the other...

Slowly flowing sky
breakup of the clouds
icebergs that have lost their way

Leaving its harp shell,
the spider crab, bungee queen,
takes the final plunge

A hammering in the streets
shutters are nailed down
the cyclone draws near

Nighttime out at sea
the shark yawns indolently,
munches a moonfish

Dancing, swaying bowls
as the tablecloth
billows in the summer breeze

Ségolène's poems, as different as they were from each other, were all alike in their form, since they always consisted of three lines: two of five syllables and one of seven, adding up to seventeen syllables, no more, no less. Always that same mysterious structure, as though governed by a code. Because Bilodo sensed that this consistency had to have a specific purpose, he'd puzzled over it until the day when, after months of foggy surmising, he happened to discover what it was all about. It was on a Saturday morning. He was having breakfast at the Madelinot while reading the entertainment supplement of a newspaper. Suddenly the sight, at the top of a page, of three written lines that seemed to form a short poem made him choke on his coffee. The poem had two lines of five syllables and one of seven. The verse was disappointing in other respects; it simply gave an ironic commentary on current affairs. It was nothing like the living fragments of eternity created by Ségolène. But the column's title was revealing: 'THE SATURDAY HAIKU'. Bilodo rushed home, combed the dictionary and found the word:

Haiku/'haiku:/ *n.* (*pl.* same) **1** a type of very short Japanese poem, having three parts, usu. 17 syllables, and often about a subject in nature. **2** an imitation of this in another language. [Japanese]

So that was it. That's what the Guadeloupean woman's poems were. Since then, Bilodo had been able to consult numerous books containing haiku at the library – books translated from the Japanese, grouping together well-known authors such as Matsuo Bashō, Taneda Santōka, Nagata Kōi and Kobayashi Issa, but none of the poems by these men produced the effect of Ségolène's, none of them carried him off to as faraway a place or made him see things as clearly or feel them as acutely.

No doubt Ségolène's penmanship contributed greatly to this exceptional magic, for she expressed herself in a more delicate, more graceful Italian hand than Bilodo had ever had the good fortune to admire. It was a rich, imaginative handwriting, with deep downstrokes and celestial upstrokes embellished with opulent loops and precise drops – a clean, flowing script, admirably well-proportioned with its perfect thirty-degree slant and flawless interletter spacing. Ségolène's writing was a sweet scent for the eye, an elixir, an ode. It was a graphic symphony, an apotheosis. It was so beautiful it made you weep. Having read somewhere that handwriting was a reflection of a person's soul, Bilodo readily concluded that Ségolène's soul must be incomparably pure. If angels wrote, surely it was like this.

4

Bilodo knew that Ségolène was a primary school teacher at Pointe-à-Pitre, and he also knew she was beautiful. He'd seen this in a picture she'd posted to Grandpré, very likely in exchange for one of his own, since the back of the photo carried this handwritten line: 'Delighted to have made your photographic acquaintance. Now it is my turn. Here I am with my pupils.' The snap showed her in the middle of a group of smiling schoolchildren, but only *her* smile mattered to Bilodo's eyes, and her emerald gaze crashed deep into his own like a wave against a cliff, reverberating there like an echo. He had digitized and printed that photo, then put it, framed, on his bedside table above the drawer where he kept her haiku. Now he could contemplate Ségolène every night before going to sleep and soon afterward dream about her: her smile, her eyes, and all the other marvels of her appearance, about romantic seaside strolls in her company, with Marie-Galante looming in the twilight and torrents of orangey clouds scudding across the sky while the wind raked their hair – unless the world of haiku got involved in his oneiric fantasies, for then he dreamt instead that he was bungee jumping with her, that they fell together at the end of an extremely long elastic before diving into a fragrant ocean, slipping between corals among moonfish and baby amphibians, amid puzzled sharks.

* * *

Bilodo was in love as he'd never imagined one could possibly be. The hold Ségolène had gained over his soul was so enormous it sometimes worried him – he was afraid his life wasn't his own any more. But the alchemical reading of a few haiku quickly transmuted his distress into bliss, and then he thanked his lucky star for favouring him like this, for having placed the Guadeloupean beauty in his path. The only shadow over his happiness was the jealousy stirring within him when he remembered that Ségolène's letters were really intended for someone else. Whenever he finished reading a new poem, he felt the sting of envy as he resealed the envelope and slipped it the next day into the slot at the apartment of that guy, Gaston Grandpré, his rival. How had he met Ségolène? What was he to her? The note on the back of the picture and the general tenor of the poems didn't suggest anything more than friendship, which cheered Bilodo up somewhat, but even so it was for Grandpré, the lucky man, that the letters were meant. Bilodo occasionally caught a glimpse of him standing in his doorway. Bearded, messy-looking, his hair unkempt, always wearing an extravagant red dressing gown, he invariably gave the impression he'd been up all night. A grouch with the air of a mad scientist about him. A grungy oddball. How did he react, Bilodo wondered, when he found another letter from her on his doormat? Did he rush to quench his thirst at the oasis of her words? Did he feel the same thrill? Did Ségolène's poems make him see things, too? The same things they conjured up for Bilodo? And what did he write in reply?

In the afternoon, when Bilodo walked past the Madelinot again on his way home, he sometimes spotted Grandpré inside, sipping a cup of coffee and scribbling in a notepad, looking inspired. Did he write poetry? Bilodo would have given anything to be able to do the same. He would have liked to reply to Ségolène's letters, just as he did to those from his other unwitting pen pals, but felt incapable of doing so, since the only way one could possibly respond to her lovely haiku was with another, just as beautifully crafted. And how could Bilodo, whom the mere word *poetry* intimidated, have managed that? Could a humble postman become a poet overnight? Could an ostrich be expected to start playing the banjo? Did snails ride bicycles? He actually tried once or twice early on and turned out a few pitiful attempts at verse, but had been overcome with shame and had never dared do it again, because he feared he might strike a blow to the very core of Poetry and indirectly tarnish Ségolène's sacred creations. Did Grandpré have that rare gift? Did he write haiku?

Was he aware at least how fortunate he was? Did he feel even a quarter of what Bilodo felt for Ségolène? Or even one-tenth?

* * *

Linked to Bilodo's worship of Ségolène was a strong fascination with the blessed land of her birth, the natural setting in the heart of which she shone. He often raided the travel shelves in bookstores and spent hours on the Internet filling his brain with anything relating to Guadeloupe: the archipelago's geology; recipes of the local cuisine; the musical tradition; the manufacture of rum; the area's history; fishing techniques; botany; architecture – he greedily lapped it all up. Little by little, Bilodo became a specialist where the 'butterfly island' was concerned, although he'd never set foot on it. He could of course have gone there, travelled there and seen Guadeloupe with his own eyes, but he had never seriously considered it because the idea unnerved him, incurable homebody that he was. Bilodo had no desire to physically visit Guadeloupe – he only wanted to get a detailed picture of it in his mind so as to feed his dreams and set them in a realistic landscape that would show Ségolène to advantage. That way he could fantasize about her in high definition, with all the necessary mental technology.

He dreamt of her cycling down the Allée Dumanoir between the royal palms that proudly lined the avenue. He dreamt of her strolling on La Darse in the afternoon when the lycée was out, or going shopping at the Marché Saint-Antoine, sauntering about in the large covered market among multicoloured stalls piled high with figues-pomme bananas and yams, sweet potatoes and chili peppers, pineapples, cherimoyas, malangas, and star fruit – not forgetting the spices, cinnamon, colombo powder, saffron, vanilla, bayberry, and curry, whose mingled aromas stirred the senses, and next to these the punches and syrups, candy and basketwork, flowers, parakeets, and brooms, beside potions, brews that bring relief and fidelity, wealth or endless love, and other magic philtres intended to cure all the ills of the world.

He dreamt of her every night, and the setting of these ethereal films, in which Ségolène played the lead, was the whole island of Guadeloupe with its winding roads and sugar-cane fields, its steep paths cutting through orchid-studded jungles dense with giant ferns, its mist-crowned mountains with strings of cascades and waterfalls dangling down the mossy, green sides. And its towering La Soufrière, dormant but ever threatening, its luminous villages with red sheet-metal roofs and cemeteries filled with black-and-white-checkered graves decorated with seashells. Its carnival, music, gwoka players, she-devils dressed all in red and other dancers in many-hued costumes wriggling their hips to the beat of bola drums while the rum flowed freely.

Guadeloupe with its mangrove swamps and guava, islands and islets, manta rays gliding on the surface of the water, its lacy coral, mullet, grouper and flying fish, the fishermen of Les Saintes, their heads shaded by *salakos*, repairing their nets. The jagged, ocean-whipped, limestone coastline of the north of Basse-Terre. Then, suddenly, surprisingly tranquil coves, blond beaches, and Ségolène swimming in the rollers of a sea as turquoise as her eyes, and the sun hastening to win back that second Venus as soon as she emerged from the waves and returned to the beach, treading it gracefully – naked and yet modest with water clinging to her breasts in beads and streaming over the downy gold of her belly.

Bilodo dreamt, and wished for nothing else; he wanted only to continue on like this, to keep savouring the dazzling dreams and ecstatic visions Ségolène's words conjured up for him. His only desire was that the pleasant status quo might endure, that nothing would disturb his quiet bliss. And nothing did, until the fateful day when the accident happened.

5

It was a stormy morning in late August. The sky hung heavy and thundered in the distance but couldn't make up its mind to spill it all out, but this didn't disturb Bilodo in the least since he had faith in the impermeability of the sturdy raincoat provided by the Post Office. At a determined pace no dreary skies could have slowed, he was making his way up and down rue des Hêtres, tackling one staircase after another, when he ran into his friend Robert, who was just transferring the contents of a postbox to his van.

They rarely met up like this, because the clearing of this particular box was generally done before Bilodo passed by, but Robert explained he had overslept after a wild night with a certain Brenda, a fantastic girl he'd met in a bar. After their hellos and some friendly banter, Bilodo wanted to get going again, but Robert held him back – he had much more to say on the subject of his brand new flame and suggested they double date that very evening with Brenda and a friend of hers, a girl with great erotic potential. Bilodo sighed. Robert's relentless efforts to set him up with a girlfriend annoyed him. His co-worker disapproved of his endless bachelorhood, considered it unhygienic, and had ironically nicknamed him 'Libido'. He'd taken it upon himself to act as a go-between and tried to mate Bilodo with anything that moved, registering him without his knowledge with online dating agencies and placing crude ads in his name along with his phone number in the sexy personal ads of trendy magazines.

All these initiatives annoyed Bilodo. He didn't dare answer the phone any more, and his voicemail was constantly clogged. But he couldn't hold it against Robert, because he knew he meant well. He was only going to all that trouble in order to help him, after all. Robert overdid it, as always, it was typical of him, but he was nevertheless the best friend he had in the world, wasn't he? Bilodo tried to appreciate him just the way he was – with his vulgarity, selfishness, hypocrisy, opportunism, compulsive exaggerating, and bad breath.

Although willing to forgive Robert for these trivial character flaws, he nonetheless hated the kind of random orgy he was being invited to. Since Robert wasn't the sort to take no for an answer, he quickly needed to come up with some valid excuse, one that wouldn't sound too lame, and that's what he was busy doing when the storm broke.

* * *

There was a sudden clap of thunder as if a colossal bag of crisps had split open overhead, and the sky cracked. The rain came down in sheets, limiting visibility to a couple of metres. Robert hurriedly flung his bag into the van and invited Bilodo to hop in so he wouldn't get soaked. The postman agreed that it would be better to let the storm blow over, so he accepted and walked around the vehicle. Just then a shout from the other side of the street drew his attention. Bilodo turned around and spotted Grandpré, Ségolène's penfriend, the man with the perennial dressing gown, on his third-storey landing exactly opposite.

Opening his umbrella, Grandpré tore down the stairs, brandishing a letter he no doubt wanted to post before Robert drove off. Bilodo watched him stepping out carelessly onto the road, which had already turned into a rising river. Without bothering to check that the way was clear, Grandpré ran towards them, hailed them, asked them to wait, and didn't see the truck coming, bearing down on them, ploughing through the downpour. Bilodo stretched out his arm, called out an inarticulate warning to Grandpré while the truck's horn blared, but it was too late. The brakes screeched, the wheels skidded on the wet road, then there was a thud. The vehicle seemed to stop instantly, as though all its kinetic energy had been passed on to

Grandpré who was catapulted into the air like a big rag doll and then crashed down with a limp thwack close to the pavement, ten metres further on.

Cars came t rue des Hêtres o a halt. The world seemed to stand still. For a few moments, the only sounds were the hum of idling motors, the crackle of the rain beating down on the asphalt and drumming on the roofs of the cars. Grandpré was now just a formless heap one could have taken for an armful of laundry that had slipped from someone's grip, if there hadn't been those shudders and dreadful spasms rocking him. Robert, the first to react, moved forward. Bilodo followed him, and they knelt down next to Grandpré, who lay there helpless, broken, his limbs bent at preposterous angles, his bushy beard spattered with thick blood that the rain, however heavy, didn't wash away. The poor guy was conscious. He stared at Robert, then at Bilodo, with a stunned look of disbelief, his eyelashes fluttering like the wings of twin butterflies, his gaze blurred by the downpour. His right hand still held the letter he'd been so eager to post, and Bilodo saw it was addressed to Ségolène.

A reddening stream rushed down the gutter. He wasn't going to make it. He desperately struggled for breath and Bilodo thought this was it, he was dying, but Grandpré began to let out odd gasps. Dumbfounded, Bilodo realised the dying man was laughing. It was definitely laughter – raucous and hollow, colourless, ghostly. Bilodo shivered and noticed he wasn't the only one: the other witnesses seemed just as disconcerted by the sinister laughter bursting forth from a dying throat. Grandpré went on laughing for a bit, as though at a painful joke. Then he stopped as he choked in a fit of coughing and spat out scarlet sputters.

Turning his head with great effort, he gazed at the bloody letter in his hand while his fingers tightened on the envelope. Grandpré closed his eyes, clenched his teeth; he looked as if he were focusing whatever strength he had left on that last expression of will, that final gesture of holding the letter. And suddenly he spoke, uttered a few words, but so faintly that only Bilodo and Robert, bent over him, could catch them: he murmured something indistinct that sounded like 'in-sole'. Then, all at once, it was the end. His eyelids opened wide and his pupils dilated, glazed over. Grandpré's eyes filled with rain, formed tiny lakes, while his last, enigmatic word lingered in Bilodo's head. What did that 'in-sole' signify? What had the dead man meant? For a fleeting moment Bilodo was tempted to look inside Grandpré's shoes to check if something was hidden there, but then he wondered if he wasn't misinterpreting the deceased's utterance. Taking into account the harrowing groans accompanying it, shouldn't one assume it to mean 'an-swer' instead – a reference to that final leap into the unknown, to that imminent dive into the mystery of the hereafter the dying man was knowingly getting ready for?

At that moment, Bilodo saw that the letter was no longer in the dead man's hand. Grandpré must have let go of it at the moment of death, and the letter had slipped into the gutter where the swift current had immediately swept it away. Bilodo spotted it drifting downstream between the feet of gaping onlookers, sucked away from the funereal circle by the whirling water as it rushed towards a sewer-grate cascade. Galvanized, he dashed after it, jostling the witnesses to the tragedy. He knew he had to get that letter back at all costs. He ran, bent down, stretched out his hand to catch it. He felt his arm grow longer, his fingers extending inordinately, and reaching it… but a millisecond too late – the sewer swallowed the letter. Carried along by his momentum, Bilodo stumbled and landed flat on his back in the cold water. A flash of lightning streaked the sky at the very moment an equally blinding realisation illuminated Bilodo: with the disappearance of that letter, which the bowels of the earth had swallowed up, his only link with Ségolène had just been severed.

6

Bilodo was in a dismal mood when he set off the next day, and it seemed to him as if the sun was in mourning, too, as if it dispensed only the cold kind of light you saw in old black-and-white movies. When he got to rue des Hêtres, he paused on the pavement, at the spot where Grandpré had fallen, and it distressed him to find that not a single trace of the tragedy remained, not even a tiny puddle of blood. The rain had washed it all away.

The haunting image of that letter gobbled up by the sewer kept returning to Bilodo's mind. He felt bad he hadn't been more alert. If only he could have caught it, read it, and found out at least what Grandpré wrote to Ségolène. Would he have posted it afterwards, he wondered? Most likely, if only to delay the inevitable. But it was no use thinking about it. Ségolène wasn't going to get that letter, so she wouldn't reply to it, and Bilodo would never again read her poems. Grandpré's death put an end to that precious correspondence, the spice of his life. Was there anything more awful than being powerless?

A little while later, as he went down the street in the opposite direction, Bilodo arrived at the door of the deceased and slipped the usual bills and advertising flyers through the letter slot, knowing full well it was pointless, the post would just pile up on the other side until perhaps a 'Request to Discontinue Service' reached the Post Office.

Pensive, he pictured the interior of that unknown apartment, where from now on silence reigned and time stagnated, where the only traces of Grandpré's earthly journey were some furniture, some objects, a few clothes hanging on motionless hangers, a few photographs, a few written works.

* * *

Grandpré's death didn't cause much commotion in the neighbourhood because people barely knew him. At the Madelinot, Tania laid a carnation on the table he usually occupied when he came in for a coffee. That was all. So this was how we departed this world, Bilodo reflected: by accident, without making waves or leaving a lingering trail, like a swallow flashing across the sky, and as quickly forgotten as a squirrel inadvertently run over on the road.

That's how it was.

* * *

Nothing appeared to have changed. Bilodo got up at dawn and went to work, had lunch at the Madelinot, then went home. His existence seemed to pursue its untroubled course, but only outwardly, for below the surface of the glassy sea that was his daily routine, a subtle change was taking place almost without him noticing.

At first, it was just a feeling of weariness, a gloomy mood he put down to the changing of the season, to the days growing shorter, a harbinger of autumn. But soon the symptoms of a deeper malaise began to show up: one night, while looking over his old clandestine correspondences, Bilodo realised that this activity, so exciting in former days, bored him all of a sudden. His favourite soap opera fell flat; none of its plots held his interest any more. The dramatic events of other people's lives no longer fascinated him.

The next day, at the Depot, he was unable to sort the post with his usual ease. He missed the target every second time, so he had to resign himself to proceeding in the conventional way. He was twenty minutes late setting off and hoped the morning air would buck him up, but he could feel his energy fading after walking just three miserable kilometres. It was even worse when he had to pit himself against the rue des Hêtres staircases: he'd merely got to the twenty-fourth one when he needed to stop to take a breather, and only reached the end of the street by a violent effort of will, after he'd allowed himself as many as six breaks. What was happening to him? Was he coming down with the flu?

When he arrived at the Madelinot, he found he had no appetite whatsoever, he who normally wolfed down his food, and ordered only vegetable soup, which he didn't even finish. He didn't bother getting out his calligraphy tools – he didn't feel like it – and immediately continued his round to make up for lost time. He was in an unusual state of mental confusion. Inattentive, preoccupied with he wasn't quite sure what, he crossed an intersection at a red light and came within an inch of being knocked over by a car. But he'd only escaped Charybdis to run into Scylla: soon after, as he dropped some advertising flyers into the letterbox of a house, Bilodo was attacked by a dog on a chain. The one-eyed animal, actually called Polyphemus according to the sign on its kennel, bit him viciously in his right calf and would only let go when its master, who'd been alerted by the howls, whacked it with a shovel. That's what happened when the gods were against you.

*　*　*

By the time the business with the dog had been dealt with – the anti-rabies vaccine administered and Bilodo's wound dressed and bandaged after he'd spent six hours at the emergency department – when that wretched odyssey had finally ended, it was late. On his way home in a taxi, Bilodo felt like doling out a few good whacks with a shovel, too. The sharp shooting pains in his leg only intensified his fury. He wanted to rebel, but what could he possibly do against the curse that had been stalking him this whole dreadful day where everything was going wrong? Once home, he bolted the door of his cocoon and hobbled up and down the living room in search of an outlet for his anger. He turned on the computer and started venting his rage on the wicked insurgents of the planet Xion. Maltreating his console, he massacred hordes of tentacular creatures, reached the game's higher level, achieved a record score, but didn't succeed in soothing the rage that twisted his guts.

Eventually he went to bed, dead tired, and found a bit of peace by gazing at Ségolène's picture. He imagined the lovely Guadeloupean woman opening her letterbox every morning, hoping to spot that reply from Grandpré, which never came. He briefly thought he might write to her to let her know her penfriend had passed away, but he couldn't do that of course – it would have meant betraying himself, admitting he'd been guilty of an indiscretion. How long would Ségolène wait, he wondered, before giving up?

* * *

It happened during the thunderstorm, on rue des Hêtres, right after the accident, but instead of Grandpré, it was Ségolène who lay helpless on the wet asphalt. She was covered with blood, dying. The young woman held out a trembling hand to Bilodo, implored him not to forget her... and he woke with a start, gasping for breath, chilled to the bone. He had trouble reconnecting with reality because the nightmare lingered, kept forcing its morbid images on him. Anxious to dispel the dread that gripped him, Bilodo spread Ségolène's haiku around him to create a defensive circle against the crawling darkness. He began reading them out loud, like so many protective incantations, but it only deepened his distress because the words refused to generate the music he expected: as soon as they were uttered, the night soaked them up, and the comforting visions they should have produced failed to appear. The haiku proved to be sterile all of a sudden. With their neatly arranged lines on their single sheets like withered flowers in a herbarium, they were lifeless, merely exuded a faded scent.

Bilodo shook the pages, hoping to reactivate the magic, but only managed to crumple them. Even Ségolène's words let him down. And at that moment, for the first time in his life, really the very first time, he felt loneliness swooping down on him. It was like a huge wave submerging him, sending him down to the very depths of himself, driving him into the darkest reaches of the ocean depths, where an irresistible maelstrom swept him towards a monstrous, gaping chasm, a gigantic sewer grate, while he groped for something to cling to, anguished to the core of his soul.

Strangely lucid, Bilodo realised he wouldn't be able to go on living without Ségolène, he wouldn't survive, nothing would have meaning or importance any more, beauty and desire lost to him forever, peace of mind an abstract concept drifting somewhere in the distance along with all those other emotions he'd probably never feel, and he himself just a piece of wreckage. A ghost ship, with no one at the helm and no power, carried along by the briny currents until eventually Sargasso weeds slowed him, caught him in their viscous nets, invading the timber, weighing him down so much he would founder in them.

What a hideous prospect. Was the story going to end so stupidly? Shouldn't Bilodo do something, try to think of something? Could the shipwreck be averted? Was there a buoy to hang on to, a way to overcome helplessness, some method or other of warding off ill fortune, of preventing Ségolène from being cast out of his life?

It was then, when his distress was greatest, Bilodo hit upon an idea.

* * *

It was a brilliant idea – original, inspired, *so* daring that Bilodo took fright and quickly put the lid back on. Because the idea was too crazy, too dangerously absurd, far too risky, and probably unworkable anyway. A wild, unwholesome idea only a crackpot could have seriously considered, which should be rejected and forgotten as quickly as possible, for fear it might proliferate. To concentrate his mind on something else, Bilodo picked up his game console and launched a violent attack on the insurgents of Xion, but the idea refused to be evicted, kept scratching under the floor tiles, demanded to be allowed to spring into the light. And finally, tired of resisting, Bilodo resigned himself to examining it again.

Perhaps the plan wasn't totally crazy after all. It was absolutely terrifying, fraught with psychological danger, but might not be impossible to carry out. If there was still a chance of re-tying the thread and finding his way back to Ségolène, *this* was definitely the way. And just when a pale new day was breaking, Bilodo looked up: he understood he had no other option, he had to at least give it a try.

7

The breaking of the window was muffled by the thick, coarse towel. Straining all his senses, Bilodo listened for some reaction from the neighbouring doors and landings, probed the darkness in the alleyway down below, but nothing stirred. He pressed against the shattered pane so the fragments fell inside. Bilodo put his hand through the hole, found the bolt, and stepped inside the door, that of Grandpré's apartment on the alleyway side, then quickly closed it behind him. He was inside. He'd done it.

A sickly sweet odour prickled his nostrils. He was in the kitchen. He switched on his torch and moved forward, making himself as light as possible, trying to levitate above the creaking floorboards. The kitchen had neither table nor chairs. The smell came from the counter; something had been left there and was rotting in its package. Fish perhaps. After crossing the kitchen, Bilodo ventured into the passageway. Its floor was covered with a soft material – not a fitted carpet but a thin mattress of some kind, which appeared to be spread over the floors of the other rooms as well. There were three doors in the passageway. The first one opened into a bedroom, the second into a small bathroom. Straight ahead lay the living room, divided in two by a large screen of some sort. Bilodo stepped around a low, oddly shaped sculpture and slipped behind the partition, finding himself in front of a writing desk next to an armchair on casters. After he'd made sure the blinds were closed, he sat down in the armchair.

The torch's beam swept the desk, revealing a computer, a calendar, a few knickknacks, a dictionary, pens, and various papers. When he examined the papers, he immediately found what he'd come for: sheets covered with writing in a hand that could only be Grandpré's. In the top drawer he made an even more exciting discovery: poems by the deceased – haiku. A whole bundle of them. And right next to those, Bilodo discovered Ségolène's, her original haiku, of which he only had copies. And her picture too!

Overwhelmed with emotion, Bilodo admired that smile, so soothing to his soul, that gentle almond gaze that always set him dreaming, then he sniffed those blessed pages Ségolène's hand had held, that her perfume still clung to, and he kissed them. One moment of such bliss was enough to justify the risks he'd taken, but the job wasn't finished: continuing his search, Bilodo explored the other drawers. What he hoped to unearth more than anything else was a rough copy of Grandpré's last letter, the one the sewer had so disgracefully swallowed up, because that was the ultimate goal of the expedition. But he'd only just begun this search when he heard voices outside, people talking on the stairs. Bilodo jumped up, switched off the torch. Just neighbours walking up to a higher floor? Or police coming to nab the despicable burglar he was? Bilodo wasn't going to wait around to find out: he stuffed as many papers as he could into his jacket and bolted, crashing into that idiotic sculpture lying about in the living room. He fled through the back door, charged down the stairs, then shot at the speed of sound towards the exit of the alleyway. He didn't dare slow down until two blocks further on, once he knew for sure he wasn't being pursued. He forced himself to walk along as naturally as possible so as not to attract attention, but his heart kept skipping, beating like a drum.

* * *

After a long shower to sluice away the sweat from the crime, Bilodo sat down at his table and reread Ségolène's haiku. He was delighted to discover that the little poems had regained their full vital power. Then, with Bill's discreet collusion, he looked over the other stolen papers, focusing especially on Grandpré's haiku, which confirmed what he'd long suspected: those two practised – had practised – a poetic exchange of some sort. Grandpré's haiku seemed quite different from Ségolène's, however. Not in form, but in spirit:

> Swirling like water
> against rugged rocks,
> time goes around and around

> Smog in the city
> it smokes far too much
> emphysema guaranteed

> They stir up the sea,
> sway the forest, draw
> a low murmur from the earth

> The rabbit's no fool
> he bursts from the hole
> where nobody lies in wait

> To break through the horizon
> look behind the set
> meet and embrace Death

It was a more sombre kind of poetry than Ségolène's, more dramatic, yet just as evocative: Grandpré's haiku made you see things too, although through a darkened lens. There were almost a hundred of them. The problem was that none were numbered. There was no indication of the order in which they'd been written or sent to Ségolène, no way of knowing which haiku was the last one, the one that never reached her.

Bilodo put the original of Ségolène's picture on his bedside table. Then, stretched out in the dark, he wondered what to do now that the first stage of his plan had been completed. Move on to phase two? Did he dare go through with his insane idea?

He fell asleep and had a strange dream. He dreamt of Gaston Grandpré, who lay dying in the middle of rue des Hêtres, just as he had in waking reality, except that the dying man didn't seem to be suffering in the least. On the contrary, he appeared to be having a good time and even gave Bilodo a knowing wink.

* * *

At dawn, when Bilodo woke up, he decided to go through with the scheme. For the first time in five years he phoned in sick to the Post Office; then, without even taking time to have a cup of coffee, he bent over Grandpré's papers and studied his handwriting, calling upon all his experience in calligraphy.

A thorough examination of the deceased's writings soon brought out an unusual feature. All over the sheets, sometimes right in the middle of a poem, a particular symbol had been drawn. It was a circle decorated to varying degrees with flourishes – could it be a stylized O? – which the author seemed to have obsessively scribbled here and there. Did that O have a particular meaning? Bilodo could only speculate. The penmanship itself was interesting, broad and vigorous. The stroke was strong, angular, boldly combining cursive and block letters, deeply scoring the paper. Pretty much the manly kind of handwriting Bilodo would've liked to have. Anyhow, he felt capable of imitating it. Choosing the same type of ballpoint pen that Grandpré had used, he made his first attempts, copying with a hesitant hand certain extracts from the deceased's poems.

The first notepad was used up shortly before noon. Bilodo's lunch consisted of a can of sardines which he ate standing as he trampled distractedly on the crumpled sheets. He set to work again, toiled until dusk, when he had to stop because of cramp. While massaging his sore wrist, he lost heart for a moment and considered giving up. But he pulled himself together at the thought of Ségolène waiting on her island and picked up his pen again, wielding it with fresh resolve.

Long after dark Bilodo finally deemed himself satisfied; he was able to produce a reasonably good imitation of the dead man's penmanship. So the second part of his plan had been completed, but he took care not to rejoice and prepared himself instead to face the next challenge, which was a sizeable one. Because the penmanship wasn't the whole story – he had to know what to write, too.

He'd deliberately avoided thinking about that aspect until then, choosing to concentrate on the task's technical side, but couldn't put it off any longer. Imitating Grandpré's hand was all very well, but, far more importantly, he needed to write what Grandpré would have written. Now Bilodo had to venture into unknown territory, into the foreign land of poetry, and manage somehow to compose a haiku that could pass as genuine in Ségolène's eyes.

* * *

His aptitude for slipping into other people's words was of no help to him in this case – when dawn broke, all he'd been able to come up with was *water*, just that one word, inspired by Ségolène's last haiku about the aquatic baby. He couldn't think of anything intelligent to add. Of course one could team it up with a variety of qualifiers: clear water, flowing water, still water. But was that really poetic? He spent the morning in a trance, struggling to join something to his *water* that would transcend it. Fire water? Running water? Sparkling water?

Waterhead?

After giving himself permission to take a brief nap, he dreamt he was drowning. He woke up just in time to fill his lungs with air and went back to the blank page. Dish-water? Holy water? Water beetle? Waterworks?

Jump into the water?

Walk on water?

Then, having become captivated by the circular movements of Bill paddling around in his bowl, he got down to it and wrote: 'A fish in water.' That was one line of five syllables already. Almost a third of the tercet.

Bilodo gazed at the words with a critical eye, then crossed them all out.

Four words, and not a single one he was happy with. At this rate, he'd still be fishing for ideas at Christmas time.

He really must speed things up. How did one go about becoming a poet, Bilodo wondered. Was it something you could learn? Maybe there was a course called Haiku 101? The yellow pages didn't list any poetry schools, so who were you supposed to contact in an emergency? The Japanese Embassy? At least one thing was becoming clear: Bilodo needed to find out more about those infuriating haiku.

8

While combing the Japanese Literature section of the Central Library, Bilodo hunted out a few highly instructive books, and it didn't take him long to learn everything he'd always wanted to know about haiku but had been afraid to ask. The principle was actually quite simple: haiku sought to juxtapose the permanent and the ephemeral. A good haiku ideally contained a reference to nature (*kigo*) or to some reality not uniquely human. Sparing of words, precise, at once complex and subtle, it shunned literary artifice and customary poetic devices such as rhyme and metaphor. The art of haiku was the art of the snapshot, of the detail. It could be about an episode in someone's life, a memory, a dream, but it was above all a concrete poem, appealing to the senses, not to ideas.

Bilodo was beginning to see the light. Even the epistolary haiku exchange Ségolène and Grandpré had practised took on a specific meaning: it was a *renku* or 'linked verse', a tradition going back to the literary contests held at the imperial court of medieval Japan.

Since Bilodo found all this fascinating and felt like talking about it, he told his friend Robert about his discoveries and read him a few haiku by Bashō, Buson, and Issa, classic masters of the genre, but the delicate balance between *fueki* – the permanent, eternity extending beyond us – and *ryuko* – the fleeting, the ephemeral that passes through us – seemed to be totally lost on the clerk, who regarded it as nothing but a sophisticated form of mental masturbation. Not that he had any prejudices against Japanese literature. On the contrary: Robert pointed out that he liked manga, those popular comic strips, but especially enjoyed *hentai*, their erotic variants, which he warmly recommended to Bilodo, whipping out a sample to back this up.

Bilodo, eager to talk to someone more capable of sharing his intellectual enthusiasm, turned to Tania. The young waitress wasn't particularly interested at first, because it was a busy time at the Madelinot. The twinkle he had expected did appear in her eyes, though, when he spread open for her the pages of a book called *Traditional Haiku of the Seventeenth Century*, a valuable publication he'd borrowed from the library, which allowed the reader to marvel at haiku calligraphed in old Japanese. Tania admitted it was very beautiful and very mysterious, very mystical. Bilodo couldn't have agreed more: combining ideograms with a phonetic syllabary, the Japanese way of writing contributed to the haiku's utter density, almost succeeded in expressing the indescribable.

* * *

The lovely goldfish,
blowing bubbles in its bowl,
swims, waving its fins

Was that poetic? Bilodo had thought at first he'd hit the bull's eye – could there be anything more Japanese than a goldfish? – but now wasn't so sure any more.

Yet he had a feeling he was on the right track, for along with 'lightness, sincerity, and objectivity', 'affection towards all living creatures' ranked among the haiku's noblest attributes. But didn't the subject itself leave something to be desired? With all due respect to Bill, was a fish the most appropriate animal for expressing poetry? Casting about for a more suitable creature, Bilodo thought of a bird, which already had the virtue of embodying 'lightness':

Tweet-tweet goes the bird
on the antenna
with a backdrop of blue sky

Was that really any better than the fish? Bilodo, upset to be so mediocre, felt his new-found self-confidence ebbing away. Knowing theoretically what a haiku consisted of was one thing, being able to write one was quite another.

Also, the literary quality was only one aspect of the problem: regardless of their debatable artistic worth, neither the fish haiku nor the one about the bird was like a poem Grandpré might have written, and *that* was their basic flaw. Most important of all, he needed to write a poem that was 'Grandpré-esque'. Bilodo had to succeed in worming his way so snugly into the deceased's mind that Ségolène wouldn't suspect anything.

* * *

It occurred to Bilodo he might do a graphological analysis of Grandpré's writings; he therefore got a book dealing with that science. He soon realised it was a discipline based on experience, an art only mastered through intensive practice, so he wondered if he'd be able to define Grandpré's personality in the short period of time available to him. In the evening, while he pored over the textbook in front of the TV, his attention was caught by comments from an actor who'd been invited to talk about his profession and explained how he'd gone about playing a famous head of state who had died a few years earlier. The performer mentioned he had begun by focusing on the great man's small gestures, his mannerisms, his ways, his habits, and had worked at copying these until eventually this process of close identification revealed to him the character's inner substance, his deepest truth. Fascinated, Bilodo closed his treatise on graphology. It struck him that what he'd just heard could be a promising lead.

At the Madelinot the next day, rather than sitting at the counter, Bilodo settled himself on the banquette Grandpré used to occupy and asked to be served what the deceased had been in the habit of ordering. Puzzled, Tania put down a tomato sandwich in front of him, which he ate while enjoying the unfamiliar view his new vantage point afforded him, not just of the restaurant but of the street beyond as well.

After lunch, while continuing his round, Bilodo carried on with the exercise by trying to imagine he was Grandpré. He closely observed the world around him, noting any incident, any detail that could give him material for a haiku. The caterpillar crawling across the pavement, for example, that openwork archway formed by intertwining tree branches overhanging the street, those squirrels bickering between the legs of a park bench, and those pink panties on a clothes line blown about by the wind – could any of it perhaps be turned into a poem?

When Bilodo reached rue des Hêtres, he leisurely strolled down the street, doing his best to see with the eyes of Grandpré, to feel what the other would have felt, and that's how it came about, when he arrived in front of the deserted apartment while trying to enter the inner world of the man who was no more, that the real way to gain access to it was suddenly revealed to him, in the form of a notice.

A red-and-black notice, sellotaped to the window, reading: 'APARTMENT FOR RENT'.

* * *

Bilodo found the owner of the building in her minuscule vegetable garden. She was a well-groomed, distrustful lady who seemed to be reassured by Bilodo's uniform. Abandoning her plants momentarily, Madame Brochu took him to the third floor and let him into the apartment which, for a change, he entered quite legally this time. How strange it was to visit that place in broad daylight after he'd slunk through it in the dark. Contrary to the sinister memory he had of it, the apartment turned out to be pleasant, well lit, remarkable mainly for its typically Japanese decoration. Bilodo couldn't have been aware of it at the time of his previous intrusion – because he had only dimly seen the premises by the glow of a torch and through the glaucous prism of stress – but the furniture, the blinds, the lamps, pretty well everything was of Japanese inspiration or style. You would almost think you had been whisked away to the land of the rising sun.

Wherever Bilodo's gaze rested, it encountered the tortured shape of a bonsai, a print, a knickknack, a statuette representing a languid geisha or a shrewdly smiling podgy bonze, a touchy samurai brandishing his sword. Those padded carpets Bilodo had found it so curious to walk on were in fact tatami mats, fitted together on the floor like pieces of a gigantic puzzle. As for that thing, that peculiar object he'd knocked over as he fled, it was actually a beautiful little table made of precious wood, delicately sculpted in the shape of a leaf bending on its stem, probably used for serving tea. On either side of the writing desk, the only Western touch present, stood a tall rack stuffed with books. The living room's second area, partitioned off by a folding paper screen painted with a mountainous landscape bright with cherry trees in blossom, must have served as a dining room. All it contained was a low table, surrounded by embroidered cushions, on which sat a tiny Zen garden.

The bedroom was plainly furnished with a futon and a wardrobe whose movable panels were fitted with tall mirrors that reflected you from head to toe. As for the bathroom, it contained a curious little wooden bath, a high, narrow vat of some sort, set right inside the regular tub, to make it easier to empty no doubt.

So Grandpré had been an enthusiast of the Japanese way of life. Not at all surprising in such an ardent devotee of haiku. That outlandish scarlet dressing gown he never took off was obviously a kimono, now probably lying in some grim cupboard at the morgue, unless it had been incinerated along with its owner.

The kitchen counter was spotless, the putrid smell no longer there – Madame Brochu had seen to it. The door's broken windowpane had been replaced. Nothing hinted that the place had recently been the scene of a burglary. Somewhat flustered, Madame Brochu explained how surprised she'd been to learn that the late former tenant, who apparently had neither heirs nor close relatives, had bequeathed his furniture and all his personal belongings to her in his will. This was an inconvenience for the dear lady, who found herself forced to dispose of the articles at her own expense, but for Bilodo it represented an unexpected stroke of luck: he suggested he rent the apartment just as it was, with everything it contained – an arrangement Madame Brochu was only too happy to accept. A few minutes later Bilodo signed his lease and received the key to his new home.

Inwardly he jumped for joy, convinced he'd finally discovered how to overcome the poetic hurdle. What better way to penetrate the mystery of Grandpré's soul than by exploring his natural habitat, by living as he himself had lived? Bilodo wandered from room to room, feeling shivers of excitement racing through him before that rich deposit of existence ready to be mined. He would go through everything, immerse himself in the premises' atmosphere, breathe in their most subtle exhalation. He would vampirize the evanescent aura of the man who'd preceded him within these walls, find out everything about him, and eventually slip so deeply into his mind that he'd have no difficulty guessing, sensing, what Grandpré would have written.

9

Bilodo didn't discover any skeletons in Grandpré's closets or any suspicious items in his fridge, nor anything particularly noteworthy in the kitchen cupboards either, except a plentiful supply of tea and several bottles of sake. He did, however, find a phenomenal number of unmatched socks in the chest of drawers as well as in the laundry hamper, and wondered what light this odorous enigma shed on the deceased's psychology. Did Grandpré steal socks from laundromats? Did he collect them? Did he turn into a centipede when the moon was full? Otherwise, the apartment contained nothing out of the ordinary.

What impressed Bilodo most was the sheer number of books on the shelves. The majority were by Japanese authors, of course. Hundreds of volumes were lined up there, bearing exotic titles and names. He opened at random a novel by a certain Mishima and came across a passage where a young woman squeezed a little mother's milk from her breast, which she then put into her lover's tea. Disturbed by such a strange gesture, Bilodo closed the book again and, deciding to complete his literary education at a later date, began to study those of Grandpré's papers that he hadn't been able to take with him the night of the break-in.

That's how he discovered a letter from Ségolène, a conventional one, entirely in prose, dating back three years. Writing to Grandpré for the first time, the Guadeloupean woman introduced herself as a lover of Japanese poetry and commented favourably on an article by Grandpré about the art of haiku according to Kobayashi Issa that had appeared in a journal of literary studies. Other letters followed. They showed how quickly an intellectual closeness had developed between them and how after a while the *renku* project was born – an idea of Grandpré's. So this was the way they became acquainted. A shared interest in Japanese literature had caused them to cross paths and strike up a friendship. At least one mystery had been cleared up.

Encouraged by this first breakthrough, Bilodo decided to take another stab at writing poetry. He had a whole weekend, since it was Friday, so he locked the door, closed the blinds, and invoked the old masters, respectfully requesting their benevolence. Then, like someone fishing for pearl oysters, he dived into his inner self.

* * *

Because Bilodo believed his previous haiku suffered from a lack of *fueki* – the eternity element – he spent all night writing a poem he meant to be a celebration of the dazzling return of dawn, finishing it in the small hours:

> The sun rises, climbs
> on the horizon
> like a big, golden balloon

It wasn't too bad, Bilodo felt. It had plenty of *fueki* anyway. But wasn't the *ryuko* content – the ephemeral or mundane element — insufficient, though? What Bilodo was aiming for was the delicate balance that characterized a good haiku, so he set to work again, making every effort to proportion these two contradictory constituents correctly.

> The sun is rising –
> I put cheese slices
> on my buttered toast

> The sun is rising
> like a big, golden navel
> on an empty gut

The sun is rising
like a golden cheese –
now let's go and have breakfast.

Bilodo noticed his stomach grumbled. Not surprising, considering he hadn't eaten anything since the day before, wrapped up as he'd been in his creative endeavour. Did one thing explain another, he wondered? Was poetry basically an affair of the stomach after all? Bilodo put the question on hold and went to have lunch at the Délicieux Orient, a local Japanese restaurant.

* * *

In the late afternoon he had a visit from Madame Brochu, who brought a fruit basket as a welcome gift. The lady noted the progress he'd made in settling in and insisted on making sure he had everything he needed. Grasping the opportunity to find out more about Grandpré, Bilodo invited her to stay for tea and served it on the pretty little leaf-shaped table. After they'd traded the usual polite remarks, Bilodo steered the conversation onto the former tenant. The dreadful circumstances of his death were recalled, commented on, deplored. Bilodo learned Grandpré had taught literature at the College nearby, but had retired the previous year although he was still quite young. Drawn out by Bilodo's keen attention, the lady revealed the poor man had behaved strangely in the last months of his life – he hardly ever left his apartment and played the same recordings of Chinese music over and over. A breakdown of some kind, she assumed, just barely able to bring herself to whisper that word of doom.

After Madame Brochu left, Bilodo drained the teapot while thinking things over. In many respects his knowledge of Grandpré's personality remained hazy, and the intricacies of his mind largely unexplored, but Bilodo was beginning to see daylight. The lady's account had added a new element:

music. Would it contribute, Bilodo wondered, to a better understanding of the man? As soon as he started rummaging through Grandpré's discs, he found the recordings of Chinese music the lady had mentioned – it was traditional Japanese music, actually. He chose one at random and put it on. The pleasing tones of a melancholy flute and chords plucked from a kind of lute filtered from the speakers, pervading the living room with a sweet recitative. Inspired all of a sudden, Bilodo grabbed his pen...

* * *

He wrote, putting on disc after disc, guzzling tea, while the shadowy hours slipped by. Arpeggios rippled from the *koto*, sometimes accompanied by a shrillish *samisen*, sometimes a *sho*, emphasizing the ethereal tone of a *hichiriki* or spellbinding nasal singing of a woman. Bilodo wrote as if in a trance, striving with his whole being towards *wabi* (sober beauty in harmony with nature), immersing himself in the age-old virtues of *sabi* (simplicity, serenity, solitude). He took an imaginary stroll through the autumnal blaze of Mount Royal and tried to render the contagious languor of the shameless trees, the rustle of leaves startled by the wind, the song of birds about to depart, and the last crunchings of insects.

He wrote, seeking the words' cooperation, struggling to seize them in midair before they scattered, to capture them like butterflies in the page's net and pin them to the paper. Every so often he achieved a line he considered tolerably good, only to decide five minutes later it rang hollow and feed it to the wastepaper basket. He'd start over, wading in a pond of crumpled cellulose, taking an occasional break to draw a hieroglyph in the sand of the tiny Zen garden or reread a certain haiku by Grandpré or Ségolène, reciting them out loud the better to admire their resonant spontaneity.

He had sushi delivered by the Délicieux Orient, which he took care to eat when Bill wasn't looking, then continued all night covering the snowy white paper with his scribbles, and all day Sunday, living on sake now, and again all evening, until his head spun, he'd developed a squint, and the pen fell from his fingers. He flopped down on the futon and sank into a sleep haunted by living ideograms and dreamt that Ségolène opened her blouse and squeezed a little milk from her breast, which she let drip between his own lips...

When he woke up on Monday morning with his neurons in a jumble, he swallowed four aspirins, took an interminable shower, then sorted through the few sheets that deserved to escape destruction and ended up choosing a poem written at twilight:

The sun is setting –
it yawns on the balcony,
snores at my window

The tercet gave off a whiff of poetry, Bilodo thought, and didn't strike him as totally foreign to what Grandpé might have written. It was almost right. But almost wasn't quite enough yet, and he methodically tore the sheet into infinitesimal pieces he sent whirling about like snowflakes. For the second time in two weeks he called the Post Office to say he wouldn't be coming in to work, then heated water for his tea and started slogging away again, determined to sacrifice an entire forest if he had to.

It was almost noon when the banging of the letterbox made him jump. Bilodo noted with a slight pang of jealousy that replacing him didn't appear to have been much of a problem and went to pick up Grandpré's post. There were two advertising flyers, one bill, and a letter from Ségolène.

* * *

It took Bilodo a moment to get a grip on himself. This was totally unexpected. He never thought Ségolène would write before Grandpré had replied to her haiku about the baby otter. With the paper knife in his trembling hand, he slit open the envelope. It contained as always only a single sheet:

Have I displeased you?
Forget the autumn
do I still have your friendship?

Bilodo felt strongly challenged by the haiku's frank, direct tone and was alarmed by the almost palpable anxiety it conveyed. Used to more punctuality from her penfriend, Ségolène obviously worried about his silence; the poor woman was afraid she had offended him in some way. Bilodo imagined her uneasiness as she wrote the poem, anxiety spreading over her lovely face, attacking its sweet fullness. That vision of Ségolène falling prey to anguish was more than he could bear, and he felt an urgent need to act. He needed to reply very quickly to reassure her and bring back her smile. Bilodo must stop dragging his feet and finally deliver that blasted haiku!

10

The grass barely filled the gaps on Gaston Grandpré's freshly sodded grave. Bilodo sank into a meditative state. Hoping to stir what was left of the deceased, perhaps his lingering soul, he silently depicted Ségolène's anxiety, the urgent nature of the situation, and stressed that his intentions were honest, his feelings sincere. Most humbly he told the man slumbering underground of his diligent efforts to imitate his works, and begged him respectfully to enlighten him: what could he do? Was there some action yet to be taken, some sacrifice he needed to agree to, some key he might have failed to insert into the complicated lock of the door barring his way to poetry?

Kneeling on the damp grass, Bilodo waited, listened with every fibre of his being, but not a single revelation issued from the grave, no sepulchral voice burst forth. Apparently the deceased had no advice to communicate. And yet...

* * *

As though in response to his visit to the cemetery, Bilodo dreamt about Grandpré that night. He dreamt in fact that he woke up and found Grandpré at his bedside, wrapped in his red kimono. The ghost was smiling in spite of the blood spattered on his pale brow, his tangled hair. His smile never fading, he moved through the room as though rolling on ball bearings. He went up to the wardrobe in this way, opened its door, and pointed at the top shelf...

Bilodo woke up in earnest. Theoretically at least. Could this be just a fractal of a deeper dream, he wondered – was he only dreaming that he had woken up – or was it real this time? Then he noticed there was no ghostly Grandpré anywhere in sight and opted for the second eventuality. He looked at the wardrobe, puzzling over the gesture the ghost had made to direct him towards the shelf. It had been just a dream, of course, but Bilodo's curiosity got the better of him and he decided to go and take a closer look, just in case. He opened the wardrobe. The top shelf was high and deep. Bilodo stretched out his hand, explored the cavity with his fingertips. He touched something. A box stowed away at the very back. Startled, he pulled it towards him. It was a black cardboard box, quite large, not very heavy, printed with Japanese ideograms. Bilodo put it on the bed and lifted the lid. Folded in thin tissue paper was a red kimono.

*　*　*

The kimono didn't look as if it had ever been worn. Bilodo took it out of the box, unfolded it. The fabric was silky, iridescent. A truly beautiful garment. Bilodo couldn't resist putting it on. To his amazement he felt perfectly comfortable in it. He took a few steps and spun around and around to see how light the kimono was. He sent the flaps flying about him – he felt a bit like Lawrence of Arabia in his first emir costume – and admired himself in the mirror. The garment moulded itself completely to his body. It looked as though it were made for him. Bilodo felt electric. It was as if a mild current flowed through his nerves, causing him to tingle all over. On a sudden impulse he left the bedroom, headed into the living room, sat down at the desk, put a blank sheet of paper in front of him, picked up a pen, placed its point on the paper. Then the miracle happened. The tip of the ballpoint started rolling over the sheet, inscribed it with a seismographic string of words. Could Bilodo still be dreaming? Inspiration had suddenly struck. It was like a dam giving way inside him, like a stalled engine finally starting. He could barely keep up with the images as they crowded into his consciousness, knocked against one another like billiard balls.

A minute later, it was finished: the mysterious force had abandoned Bilodo, leaving him haggard, worn out. Before him lay a haiku. It had written itself, in one go, without a single deletion, automatically, in handwriting one would have sworn was Grandpré's:

Perpetual snow
on lofty heights, unchanging
such is my friendship

Bilodo tried to make sense of what just happened; he thought it might be a conditioning phenomenon of some kind, the catalyst of which had been the discovery of the kimono. Putting on the garment, slipping symbolically into Grandpré's skin had probably triggered the creative process he'd been trying to start for days. Or was it spiritualism? Had Bilodo been briefly possessed? Had Grandpré's spirit granted his wish so as to help him? Bilodo felt too shaken to decide. The important thing was the poem: whether under spiritual influence or not, Bilodo had just written what he thought was the first good haiku of his life. Would it succeed, though, in comforting Ségolène? Would it appeal to her?

Bilodo folded the paper and slipped it into an envelope. But just as he was about to close it, he hesitated, tormented by one last dilemma: should he add that stylized O to the haiku – the one Grandpré used to draw on everything? Was it some kind of signature or graphic seal, the absence of which might arouse suspicion? To find out, he would have needed to examine the deceased's previous mailings; once again the loss of Grandpré's last letter made itself sorely felt. Bilodo finally chanced forgoing it. He sealed the envelope and hurried to post it before he changed his mind.

It would take five or six days for the haiku to reach Ségolène and at least as many for her reply to get back to him – supposing that she replied, that she didn't suspect the deception, that the ruse worked.

* * *

The letter arrived eleven days later. Bilodo had been hoping for it with all the passion he had inside him, praying for it constantly, no longer daring to touch his pen or put on the kimono for fear of jeopardizing fate's delicate balance, but there it was at last, in his hand, as he stood transfixed at his counter in the Depot. Unable to wait, he rushed to the men's room, locked himself in the last cubicle, tore open the envelope, and read:

Sheer, towering peaks
respectful regards from your
humble mountaineer

Bilodo was instantly transported into a Himalayan landscape worthy of *Tintin in Tibet*. Clinging to a rock, he stood halfway up a steep, downhill slope of virgin snow, dazzling in the harsh sunlight, while ahead of him rose the summit, far off and yet close by in the rarefied air, sharply outlined against the deep blue sky, moody, imperious in its rugged grandeur...

When after all that time Bilodo finally savoured Ségolène's words again, he felt invigorated, strong as a yeti. It was like a transfusion after a haemorrhage, a puff of oxygen when you are suffocating. He jubilated in the washroom. It had worked! She had believed in it!

Some austere mountains
secretly hope that at last
someone dare climb them

They act tough, flaunting
their avalanche clothes,
but they are tender-hearted

They are scared at night
weep with loneliness
their tears create waterfalls

This is how mountain
lakes pool into existence
in icy silence

* * *

Bilodo felt his happiness was complete. What more could
he want? The kimono hung waiting for him in the wardrobe,
but he was careful not to use it too often; he saved it, donned
it only when it was time to reply to Ségolène. Then all he needed
to do was put the miraculous garment on and his soul took
wing, whizzed away, while colours and visions came rushing
in. Bilodo had finally rejected any kind of supernatural explanation for the phenomenon. He reckoned that his discovery of
the kimono right after the dream about a ghostly Grandpré
was simply a fortunate coincidence, and as for the rest, that
was just the subconscious manifesting itself. Besides, he didn't
really want to delve more deeply into the issue, because he
feared that being too inquisitive might slow down his creative momentum and jeopardize the poetry. The basic cause of

the miracle wasn't particularly important to him, as long as it worked and he could keep writing to Ségolène, as long as he could dream about her playing the flute on the bank of the lazy river, charming snakes as in that painting by Henri Rousseau, then dozing on a bed of greenery while wildflowers wrapped her in live petals and forest animals mounted a jealous guard by her side.

* * *

Shimmering forms – dawn
through half-closed lashes
iridescent theatre

A flower flies from
the hair of the fruit vendor
it's a butterfly

Mini-monster commandos
haunting the pavements
on Halloween night

A runaway horse
he looks terrified!
what's biting him, I wonder?

Crystal-glazed puddles
the grass crunches underfoot
another winter

My big cat purrs on the bed –
right under his nose
the mouse scampers off

The perfect beauty
the divine architecture
of a soft snowflake

Enormous black backs
whip up the ocean –
the sperm whales are frolicking

* * *

She swam and gambolled, enormous, yet so nimble. Her dark, streamlined body undulated gracefully, stood out against the sunlight on the shimmering screen of the surface, skimming the sparkling curtain, sometimes cleaving it with her back. She swam and melodized, she filled the ocean with her songs, because she was a whale. And so was he. They were whales and swam together, they were heading over yonder, to that place that had no name, that was simply 'over yonder', far off in the infinite blue expanse. They were in no hurry. They dawdled, glided in a muted twilight glow. They would hunt a little, then let themselves be carried along, trusting the currents. They'd come up now and again to blow out a geyser of iodized steam and fill their lungs with air, to drift for a spell, swaying gently with the waves, then they'd go down again to where it was calm.

It was good to be a whale. It was good to be with her, just with her, and be free together. If he had had a choice, he would rather have been the ocean so he could have hugged Ségolène even more closely, and put his endless water arms around her everywhere at once, and slid all over her skin forever, but even so it was nice to be a whale. It was a great joy, as long as she was there and together they could escape time.

Now she sounded all of a sudden. She went into a nosedive, fled from the light. Had she detected an appetizing prey? Was it just for the fun of getting to the bottom of things, of exploring some unfamiliar wreck, or was she playing hide-and-seek? He followed her, plunging with powerful strokes of his tail; he wasn't going to lag behind. He dived after her to where the darkness deepened, surrounded you, held you in an ever tighter, ever colder grip. He had already lost sight of her but could feel the vibrations of the mass of water she displaced, and he heard her sing in the gloom close by. She was calling. She was calling *him*, and he answered, also with a song, because that was how you communicated when you were a whale – you sang into the void, unafraid of the darkness that grew ever darker, ever deeper.

12

A kid is shouting
he's waving his stick about
he just scored a goal

The little girl screams
On the window ledge
she has seen a centipede

On the clothes line in the yard
the washing freezes
and sparrows shiver

My neighbour Aimée
gardens in a floral dress
You would water her

* * *

January was wreaking its havoc. It had already been three
months since Bilodo moved into Grandpré's place. He now felt
perfectly at home there but continued to think 'at Grandpré's
place'. It was automatic, but also a mark of respect for the man
to whom he owed so much happiness. He only went over to his
old apartment when it suited him, to pick up his scanty post
and delete from his voicemail the smutty propositions that kept
flooding into it. His furniture and most of his things were still
there. He had hardly moved anything into Grandpré's place, not
wanting to alter its pleasing Oriental atmosphere. He could have
sublet his old apartment now that he didn't need it any more,
but had decided not to, because he used that official address
as both a cover and an alibi so as to preserve the tranquillity of
the parallel life he led in his lair on rue des Hêtres. That way,

he didn't have to fear either visits from unwelcome guests or ill-timed intrusions by Robert. Bilodo hadn't told the clerk anything, and the mere thought of him turning up with his huge clogs in the muffled seclusion of his Japanese sanctuary made him shudder. Robert, who was no fool, suspected something, of course. It struck him as odd that Bilodo never answered the phone and was never home when he stopped by. Robert's questions were becoming embarrassing and Bilodo found it more and more difficult to evade them.

Apart from Robert's nosy queries, the outside world rarely intervened in Bilodo's cloistered life, centred completely on his imaginary romance. There was Tania, at the Madelinot, who never missed an opportunity to gab and ask how his research into Japanese poetry was coming along. As a matter of fact, Bilodo had got into the habit of devoting his lunch break, after dessert, to the revision of haiku he meant to send to Ségolène, and Tania, puzzled, often asked him what he was writing and if she could read it. He refused as nicely as possible, on the pretext that it was too personal, but the young waitress continued to show a keen interest in his writings, which was rather touching. He was sorry he always had to say no to Tania. And because he wanted her to like him, he promised he'd write a haiku especially for her one day. She seemed thrilled.

Apart from that, Bilodo saw practically no one. There was Madame Brochu, with whom he exchanged the occasional polite remark, although more briefly since a recent incident: when she came knocking at his door to ask him to turn down the volume of his Chinese music, the lady had looked shocked at seeing him wearing Grandpré's kimono. She had been less cordial after that and eyed Bilodo suspiciously ever since. It was understandable, he thought. Judged from the outside, his behaviour was certainly surprising. Judged from the inside as well: living the way he did, having slipped into someone else's mind and clothing, surely denoted a high degree of eccentricity. But he fully accepted being odd in this respect, no matter what other people might think. The important point was never to lose sight of the deeper logic.

* * *

A wandering man
found frozen to death
on a bench, today at dawn

*La Soufrière – its
head in the clouds as though in
elevated thoughts*

It's been snowing hard
thirty centimetres now
snow-blower heaven

*Vidé touloulou
It's the Grand brilé Vaval
ti-punch flows freely*

* * *

Vidé, in Creole, was a parade, a procession, because in Guadeloupe, too, it was the end of February, carnival time. *Touloulou* was a dance for which the ladies enjoyed the privilege of choosing their partners, while *Vaval* was the king of the festival, the local mascot, sort of the Bonhomme Carnaval of the area. The *Grand brilé* was a popular ceremony that took place on the evening of Ash Wednesday and concluded the carnival with the burning of the unfortunate Vaval amid cries and wails from the hysterical crowd. As for the freely flowing *ti-punch*, that was clear enough. Bilodo supposed it was probably all very much like the Quebec Carnival, but fifty degrees warmer.

Eager to share Ségolène's festive mood and show her that celebrations around here were every bit as joyful as the ones on her island, he sent her a rousing:

Swing your partner round and round
gents fall back one and
swing the girl behind!

And he, who had never set as much as a toe on a dance floor, dreamt that night that he whirled around merrily with Ségolène in the unlikely, highly diverse setting of a festive town that was a cross between Vieux-Québec and Pointe-à-Pitre. He dreamt that they danced now a frenzied rigadoon on the icy pavement of Place d'Youville, now a wild gwoka in the fragrant sultriness of Place de la Victoire. And Ségolène laughed and twirled around, never tiring, her hair whipping the night.

13

On the first Monday in March a parcel arrived from France, addressed to Gaston Grandpré. It contained a manuscript called *Enso*, which was written by Grandpré himself and had an illustration of a black circle with a frayed outline on the cover page. That mysterious circle again, the O that showed up on all of the deceased's papers.

With the document came a short letter from the editor of a free-form poetry series published by Éditions du Roseau in Paris. The editor acknowledged the work had certain good qualities, but he regretted he was unable to accept it for publication. Bilodo leafed through the manuscript, a mere sixty or so pages, each containing a single haiku. He wasn't really surprised to discover that the opening poem of the collection was well known to him:

Swirling like water
against rugged rocks,
time goes around and around

The following haiku were familiar to him as well: he had read them many times, sometimes in versions somewhat dissimilar to those he now had before him:

They come from the east,
gulls screeching like witches at
a midnight revel

A steep granite spine
wild tangle of spruce
and then at long last the beach

Magnificent sweep
Oh! the utter perfection
of that golfer's swing!

His driver of light
sending the ball soaring high
up among the stars

Having only dipped into Grandpré's haiku in a random fashion until now – perusing a poem here and there among the man's chaotic papers – Bilodo found it to be a very different experience to read them in the particular order in which the author had placed them. Their specific sequence gave them a kind of incantatory power. As Bilodo turned the manuscript's pages, he had the impression he was heading towards a hidden goal, that he moved in spite of himself towards an implacable fate. The haiku resonated against one another, producing a music of the mind with a haunting rhythm. They gave him an archetypal sensation of déjà vu, of having experienced or, rather, dreamt it all before. They stirred up old images in deep strata of his memory.

In the ocean depths
gloom is a meaningless word
Down there the light kills

Ribcage perfectly
picked clean, the march of
necrophagous centuries

To break through the horizon
look behind the set
meet and embrace Death

Rejoice, mermaids and mermen,
the Prince of the Deep
has returned to you

Dark and yet luminous, the haiku followed one another, a procession of pelagic fish exuding their own phosphorescence. The collection's title puzzled Bilodo; he looked up the word *Enso* in the dictionary but couldn't find it. Falling back on the Internet, he had the satisfaction of seeing many references displayed on the screen, all showing circles similar to the one on the cover page, and discovered this to be a traditional symbol in Zen Buddhism. The *Enso* circle represented the emptiness of the mind allowing one to attain enlightenment (*satori*). Having been painted by Zen masters for thousands of years, it prompted a spiritual exercise in meditation on nothingness. The circle, drawn with a single continuous brushstroke – without hesitating, without thinking – was believed to reveal the artist's state of mind: one could only trace a powerful, well-balanced *Enso* when one's mind was clear, free of all thought or intention.

As he tried to find out more, Bilodo learnt that the Zen circle could be interpreted in numerous ways: it could represent just as well perfection, truth, or infinity, simplicity, the cycle of the seasons, or the turning wheel. On the whole, *Enso* symbolized the loop, the cyclical nature of the universe, history always repeating itself, the perpetual return to the starting point. It was similar in that sense to the Greek Ouroboros symbol, depicting a serpent biting its own tail.

Enso, a rich and diverse symbol, and a title that took on its full, definitive meaning when one reached the manuscript's last page, which contained the same haiku as the collection's first page:

Swirling like water
against rugged rocks,
time goes around and around

The repetition couldn't possibly be accidental. Grandpré had meant it this way; he had given his collection the shape of a loop. The return to the opening poem, which itself evoked the loop, was *Enso*, the Zen circle, the book perpetually repeating itself.

Lost in thought, Bilodo closed the manuscript. He regretted it had been rejected by the publisher. The work brought together Grandpré's best poems, his most accomplished ones, and it being turned down like this seemed unfair: the guys at that publishing house were obviously asleep at the wheel. But they weren't the only publishers in the world after all. Checking the Web once more, Bilodo got a list of the leading publishers of Quebec poetry and made a decision: he was going to submit the manuscript elsewhere. *Some*one *some*where was sure to see the light.

He would get the collection published. It was a posthumous duty he felt entrusted with. Wasn't it the least he could do to honour the memory of Grandpré – the pioneer who had blazed a trail for him that led to Ségolène?

14

On the canoe floor
a suffocating trunkfish,
drowning in the air

Being a frog and
breathing through the skin,
truly the best of both worlds

Raindrop on the leaf,
for a ladybug
a natural disaster

The faithful master
leans over and scoops
Who is really on the leash?

La Désirade's waves
clear and luminous
like a tanka by Bashō

* * *

Bilodo had grown somewhat familiar with Bashō, that fine haiku poet of the seventeenth century, but just what was a *tanka* again? He knew the word. He remembered coming across it during his literary explorations the previous autumn.

It didn't take him long to track it down in Grandpré's books. The tanka was the oldest, most elevated classical Japanese verse form; its art had been practised exclusively at the Imperial Court. It was the haiku's ancestor, the venerable forefather the haiku descended from. It was a more extensive poem, having five lines rather than three, and consisted of two parts: the first one, a tercet of seventeen syllables, was simply that good old haiku, while the second, an added-on distich made up of two lines of seven syllables each, responded in some way to the first and gave the stanza a new direction. Bilodo learnt that either form had its own, particular subject area. Unlike the haiku – a brief poem speaking to the senses and tending to involve the observation of nature – the tanka was meant to be lyrical, exquisite, refined. Its practitioners strove to explore noble themes and sentiments such as love, loneliness, death. The poem was devoted to the expression of complex emotions.

Bilodo shivered. What did that allusion by Ségolène to the tanka mean? Was it a subtle message, an invitation?

A form favouring the expression of feelings. Wasn't that precisely what Bilodo longed for? Hadn't he felt constricted at times by the limitations the haiku imposed on him? Wasn't he tired, quite frankly, of evoking weather reports, clothes lines, and little birds? Hadn't the time come to contemplate grander, more beautiful things and break out of the tight, binding garment? Didn't he feel the desire to go further, to finally lay bare his heart?

Bilodo slipped on his kimono, then started writing, eager to experiment with the unfamiliar form, and was surprised to find he had no trouble coming to grips with it. The stanza materialized all by itself, dropped into his hands like a ripe fruit:

Some flowers, it seems,
take seven years to open
For a long, long time
I have wanted to tell you
how intensely I love you

Proud of his first tanka, euphoric, Bilodo rushed out to post it. It wasn't until later, once his adrenalin level had gone back to normal, that he began to reflect on what he'd done and doubt crept into his mind.

Was it wise – if you really thought about it – to send Ségolène a poem so different from the ones she usually received? It wasn't the form he worried about but the content: how would the young woman react to the explicit declaration, this sudden intrusion in the formerly reserved sphere of feelings? Might it not alienate her? Would the sweet, subtle bond between them not suffer by it? Hadn't Bilodo been too bold?

He now regretted acting so impetuously, but the harm was done: the tanka lay at the bottom of the postbox on the other side of the street, irretrievable. In theory, at least. Wasn't Robert, whose duties included collecting the post, supposed to show up towards noon?

Not long before that time, Bilodo went out to wait for Robert, walking up and down past the postbox like a neurotic sentry, deaf to the warbling of birds another April brought back from the south. Finally, after half an hour, the van appeared. It drew up alongside the pavement and Robert got out with loud whoops of delight at finding his old pal Libido there. Cutting the outpouring short, Bilodo explained the favour he expected from his friend. Robert appeared reluctant at first, arguing that what Bilodo asked of him was highly irregular, but it was just to keep him in suspense for a bit – how much weight did a few stupid regulations really carry compared with the unbreakable brotherly bond uniting them?

Once he'd relieved the postbox of its contents, the postal clerk had Bilodo get into the van with him, and there, safe from the rabble's prying eyes, he emptied his bag, invited Bilodo to fish out that famous letter he said he'd posted by mistake. While mumbling incoherently from sheer gratitude, Bilodo spread about the various parcels, envelopes, used syringes, stolen hockey jumpers, and other vile things the box had excreted, and found his letter. All danger was passed now, and

Bilodo felt relieved, although vaguely disappointed, without quite knowing why. Robert's snooping eyes had nevertheless deciphered the address on the envelope. Since the clerk hadn't believed Bilodo's lame excuse for a minute and sensed there might be a woman behind all this, he demanded to know who that Ségolène was Bilodo was writing to in Guadeloupe. Bilodo instinctively concealed the letter in his jacket. Grateful as he might be to Robert, he refused to talk, stated it was strictly confidential. Contrary to expectation, Robert didn't push the matter, but warned his friend he wouldn't be let off the hook without at least going for a drink with him after work, to celebrate. Bilodo hesitated, knowing how easily an invitation of this sort could lead to things getting out of control, but after what Robert had just done for him, how could he refuse?

15

Bilodo dreamt he heard someone laughing. As he woke up, it took him a minute to realise he was lying fully dressed on the futon with the blinds open and the morning sun stamped right onto his face. He tried to get up, then abandoned the idea, floored by a throbbing ache boring into his skull. The memory of last night's excesses came back to him in snatches. There was that pub on rue Ontario where the night out began, those glasses of Scotch appearing one after the other at the bar. What came next was already a bit blurred: there was that club with female dancers on the rue Stanley, also a cubicle where sensual beauties swayed their hips in close-up, then the massage parlour Robert had dragged him off to against his will, then that Hawaiian pizza ingested on a banquette in a glaringly bright restaurant, then yet another place – a bar? a club? – but he had absolutely no recollection of what came after.

And there were those questions. Those indiscreet questions from Robert who quizzed him again and again about the letter, about Ségolène, and relentlessly returned to the charge as the night wore on, as things got more and more out of hand. The clerk had obviously meant to take advantage of his alcoholic stupor to get the full lowdown. What had Bilodo let slip? He had to admit he had no idea. What did he tell Robert? What had happened during those black bits that hatched the mental film of the night?

The laugh he'd heard in his dream rang out again, except that Bilodo was wide awake this time. It came from the next room. Someone was laughing in the living room. With a shock Bilodo recognised Robert's distinctive braying and realised the clerk was right there, in the adjoining room. A squirt of fresh memory data splashed onto his mind: he suddenly remembered that after the wild spree, in the small hours of the morning, he had stupidly let his friend drive him home. His new home! His secret refuge!

He recalled Robert's drunken amazement when he found out the little sneak had moved without telling anyone, and then his surprise when he discovered the Japanese décor of Bilodo's new lair. He recalled how his friend had explored the premises, looking for a geisha, drained a bottle of sake, pissed in the bathtub, knocked over the little tea table, then collapsed on the tatami and snored like a B-52 in search of a city to drop an atom bomb on. Bilodo's migraine flared up. What an unforgivable blunder! Now the secret of his private fortress was out. Robert knew. He was right there, in the living room, and he was laughing. What could he be finding so funny?

Bilodo managed to get up in spite of his seasickness and navigated his way into the corridor. Another burst of laughter from Robert. Bilodo held on to the wall and reached the doorway to the living room, where he found Robert in his boxer shorts and undershirt slouched in the armchair at the desk. He was reading something he obviously thought highly comical. And that thing was a haiku by Ségolène.

The drawer was open. The young woman's poems were scattered about on the desk and Robert had a few of them in his hand, defiling them with his sacrilegious gaze while he scratched his scrotum and even had the gall to recite them in his croaking Pithecanthropus voice.

'"*They act tough, flaunting / their avalanche clothes / but they are tender-hearted,*"' Robert said, guffawing. 'In *those* clothes I guess they'd call a blow job a *snow* job.'

At the sight of the clerk in his underwear holding Ségolène's refined poems between his fat, disgusting fingers, sullying them with his glowering stare and coarse laugh, Bilodo felt his blood turning to ice in his veins. In the toneless voice of a robot about to break the First Law, he ordered Robert to give the sheets back to him, but Robert seemed in no hurry to comply.

'Wait,' he said, flipping through the poems. 'The other ones are even lousier.'

And the clerk did it again, read another haiku in a ridiculous falsetto voice. Bilodo moved towards him. Robert had expected that. He jumped out of the chair and ran to the other end of the room. Bilodo pursued him, determined to get the precious poems back no matter what. He finally outwitted the miserable clown's manoeuvrings and managed to catch hold of them, but that idiot wouldn't let go, so the inevitable happened… Bilodo stared, bewildered, at the fragments of the torn sheets Robert still clutched, and then at the ones in his own hand.

'Oops!' said Robert, roaring with laughter.

'Get out,' Bilodo ordered in a monotone.

'Relax,' the clerk shot back defiantly. 'Let's not get all worked up about three or four shitty poems!'

Did he really say 'shitty'? As swiftly as it had solidified, Bilodo's blood liquefied, instantly reaching the boiling point. His fist clenched, lashed out, punched Robert on the nose. The clerk was hurled through the cherry trees on the folding screen and crashed down on the low table behind it. Bilodo snatched the shreds of paper from between his fingers. Dazed, holding his bloody nose, the clerk picked himself up as best he could and had the nerve to take it badly. He swore, flailed his arms, tried to strike back, but his blow only grazed his co-worker's ear. Bilodo retaliated by planting a hefty right in his belly. Robert deflated, all the aggressiveness draining out of him along with the air in his lungs. Bilodo took advantage of it to pick him up by his vest, and dragged him to the hallway, just barely taking time to open the door before heaving him out. Robert, flung out onto the staircase, bounced down three steps on his backside. Bilodo threw his clothes at him and bolted the door.

He couldn't believe it. He who had never hurt a fly without regretting that he couldn't give it an anaesthetic first had just hit his best friend. His ex-friend, that is. But he had a more pressing concern right now. It was a serious moment: some of Ségolène's loveliest haiku were in shreds. Indifferent to the insults and dire warnings Robert was uttering outside, as well as his violent banging on the door, Bilodo got out a roll of sellotape and applied himself to piecing the treasured sheets together again. Behind the door Robert had begun to make threats, swearing he wasn't going to get away with it, he'd get his own back sooner or later, but Bilodo didn't hear a thing, engrossed as he was in the delicate surgical operation of mending the mutilated verse.

It wasn't until later – long after Robert's shouts had died away, once Ségolène's poetry had been fully restored – that Bilodo realised, as he searched in his jacket pocket for the unsent letter he'd slipped into it the previous day, that it wasn't there any more. It had vanished along with the tanka it contained.

He had no recollection of what he might have done with it. Had he foolishly mislaid it during last night's cavorting, or had that scumbag Robert swiped it?

16

When Bilodo walked into the Madelinot at lunchtime, he noticed Robert sitting with the inevitable band of colleagues in the postal workers' spot. The swelling and abnormal hues of his nose were hard to miss. Bilodo felt a volley of hostile looks focusing on him; Robert had obviously circulated a highly biased version of the nasal attack. Bilodo tried to ignore the prevailing animosity. He took a seat at the counter. Tania came over to put a bowl of soup down before him and, as he began spooning it up, he pondered how to tackle the tricky business of the filched tanka. Did Robert actually have it in his possession? Putting the question to him point-blank was unthinkable, especially in front of the others. How could he find out, he wondered, without compromising himself, or running the risk the clerk might somehow take advantage of the situation? And, should it be necessary, how could he get the letter back without being forced to eat humble pie and apologise to him, or even worse, depending on how foul his mood was? Bilodo absently chewed his shepherd's pie, hoping Robert would clarify things himself by coming over and naming the amount of the ransom, but it didn't happen: there was nothing in the clerk's attitude that led one to believe he might have any other intention towards Bilodo than to hate him until the end of time.

After lunch, as he stepped out of the men's toilets, he almost collided with Tania, who stood right there, beside the door, waiting for him. Beaming, the young woman said she wanted to thank him. For the poem, of course. And Bilodo saw she had a sheet of paper in her hand. The tanka!

Her eyes moist with happiness, Tania explained how pleasantly surprised she'd been to find the poem on the counter, along with the bill and the money owing. She confessed she was deeply touched by it, and modestly lowered her gaze before adding with a blush that she felt the same way. Bilodo, dumb-founded, finally understood: she thought the tanka was for her, that he'd written it for her as promised, and that… This was so horrific it took his breath away. He couldn't string two coherent words together, and even less shatter Tania's illusions; all he could manage was an inane smile. The young woman, who must have put his confusion down to shyness, was tactful enough to drop the subject, and merely looked at him one last time with shining eyes before going back to work.

Bilodo breathed again. The situation hadn't only overtaken him – it now had a one-lap lead. No need to look too far for the perpetrator of this vile plot: down at the other end of the restaurant, Robert's fiendish smile was explanation enough. How the son of a bitch gloated over his revenge! Bilodo grabbed his jacket and slipped out, but not without answering Tania's little wave full of thrilling hidden meanings. Enraged, he went to wait for Robert near his van.

The clerk showed up ten minutes later. Still sporting that jubilant grin that was his odious speciality, Robert asked when the wedding would be. Bilodo bristled with anger as he reproached him for deceitfully involving Tania in a disagreement that concerned only them. Robert sardonically assured him he'd just wanted to make Tania happy, although he'd never understood why she was so crazy about a stupid bastard like him. Stupid, yes, Bilodo agreed he really must be pretty dense for not having noticed sooner what a filthy pig Robert was. The clerk snapped back that was still better than being a moronic asshole and warned Bilodo he had seen nothing yet, from now on it was open war between them. Following which he took off like a shot.

Because Bilodo knew from having seen Robert in action how implacable he could be when he wanted to, he spent the rest of the day worrying about the various forms, each one more harrowing than the next, his threats were likely to take. With respect to Tania in any case, one thing was certain: no matter how disappointing this might be for her, he had to tell her the truth.

* * *

Robert's threats didn't take long to materialize. When Bilodo arrived at the Depot the next day, he spotted with utter dismay on the staff lounge notice board a photocopy of his tanka carrying his forged signature; it had been printed on pink paper for greater visual impact. Other copies had been distributed all through the centre, particularly in the sorting cubicles, from which peals of laughter rang out. The whole world seemed to have read his poem. It was the joke of the day: anyone running into Bilodo put in their two cents' worth with some little allusion to love, to flowers, or to horticulture in general. Since there was nothing to be done about it, the postman took refuge in an aloof silence, stoically enduring the snub. When he could finally leave for his round, it felt like a release, but a fast three-hour walk was barely long enough to settle his nerves.

Shortly before noon Bilodo headed towards the Madelinot, his mind firmly made up to speak to Tania, tell her the truth, but when he walked into the restaurant he realised Robert's machinations had preceded him: no one would look at him and conversations died as he went past, except in the postal workers' corner, where there was open sniggering around Robert, who had a malicious look in his eye and whose nose had turned purplish. When Tania saw him, she acted as if she didn't know him and disappeared into the kitchen.

'Ségolène! Ségolène!' the buffoons wailed languorously at the other end.

Bilodo blanched. Right then he would have given anything to be on the other side of the world. He almost turned on his heel, then remembered he must talk to Tania first, and courageously walked on. Braving the bleatings, puns and other subtle poetic allusions, he went to sit at the counter.

'Ségolène! Take me in your sloop to Guadeloupe!'

Bilodo clenched his fists, not sure how long he'd be able to bear it. Tania came out of the kitchen again with a tray of food. He signalled to her, but she ignored him completely, bringing the postal workers their meals instead. That group wasn't going to let such a wonderful opportunity of teasing her slip by and asked her if she planned to spend her holidays in Guadeloupe this year, if she wasn't too jealous of her rival, if she didn't mind being part of a ménage à trois, and then pointed out that her fiancé, Libido, was waiting for her at the counter and if she hurried, she might end up with another wonderful love poem, just for *her* this time. Tania finished serving them without saying a word but was obviously fuming. Finally she seemed to think she'd let Bilodo stew long enough, and appeared on the other side of the counter to take his order, so icy she could have sunk a dozen *Titanic*s. What could she get him? Duck – another sitting duck like her? Or a nice little goose, perhaps? A guinea pig to test a new poem on? Deeply apologetic, Bilodo replied she'd got it all wrong, he needed to talk to her in private, but the waitress answered there was no point to that, there was nothing more to say, and she threw a ball of crumpled paper on the counter.

'Here's your poem, Libido!' she spat out.

Clapping broke out in the postal workers' corner and in the rest of the room as well, because Tania definitely had supporters: the entire lunch crowd was following the action with interest. Bilodo pursued the waitress all the way to the kitchen doors, swearing to her in a low voice that it wasn't his fault, the poem hadn't been written for her and should never have been given to her, but Tania, who exuded distrust, wanted to know why he hadn't told her this the day before, instead of letting her make a fool of herself. She then put a stop to Bilodo's mumblings by saying she didn't want to hear about their sick little games any more: let him and Robert find another victim and leave her alone. Another round of applause backed up this rousing command.

Bursting into tears, Tania took refuge in the kitchen, and was replaced in the doorway by Mr Martinez, the establishment's cook, who weighed a good 130 hostile kilos, not counting his kitchen knife. Bilodo saw no option but to retreat, and he dashed out of the place where he was now nothing but an outcast. He wanted to flee as quickly as he could and go and hide at the ends of the earth, but the street swayed under his feet; his legs failed him, and he had to sit down on the steps of the first staircase he came across so as not to collapse.

Five minutes later he was still there, struggling against a feeling of helplessness, doing his best to overcome it, to digest the acidic brew of shame and anger churning in his guts, when the postal workers emerged from the Madelinot, led by Robert. The clerk walked past him, visibly enjoying the sad sight of Bilodo's downfall, and kept going, triumphantly escorted by his minions, who struck up a hymn dedicated to the exotic beauties of the Guadeloupean archipelago. Too weak to protest, Bilodo lowered his eyes and sat staring at the folds of the crumpled tanka he still held in his hand... Then he looked more closely and smoothed it out, noticing suddenly it wasn't the original but another photocopy! Galvanized into action, he called Robert, who was already a hundred metres ahead with his henchmen. The clerk consented to wait for Bilodo as he ran to catch up with him. The time to be subtle being long past, Bilodo demanded Robert give him back his letter. The clerk appeared greatly amused by the request and replied he didn't have his crappy poem any more, he'd simply posted it, then he walked off surrounded by his pack. Bilodo stood stock-still, paralyzed by what he'd just heard: the tanka was on its way.

After all these tribulations, he was back at the starting point. *Enso.*

17

The tanka was travelling inexorably towards Ségolène, and all other concerns had been swept away. Robert's schemes, Tania's heartache, the Post Office, life, death – none of it mattered any more to Bilodo. Had she received the poem? Had she read it? Was she shaken, stunned? Bored, disappointed, scornful? Or quite the opposite: had it touched her, delighted her and was everything perfectly fine? Because Bilodo wanted to favour the second assumption, he found the memory of Tania's initial reaction when she'd read the tanka reassuring: it augured well for Ségolène's response, didn't it? Then the judgement Robert had passed on the poem sprang into his mind and he wasn't sure of anything any more. 'Crappy!' the clerk had said. Could he, by some terrible fluke, be right? Bilodo had nightmares about it. In his dreams he saw gigantic lips part and contemptuously utter the word: 'Crappy.'

And those lips were Ségolène's – those ferociously red lips, those white predatory teeth, that pitiless mouth repeating the murderous word: 'Crappy.'

And each time it was like a dagger through his heart, because he knew it to be true, his poem was crappy, and she was absolutely right to say it again to punish him for his foolishness. And Ségolène's teeth tore the tanka into a thousand pieces that flitted in all directions, scattering to the furthest reaches of cold nothingness, and on those bits of paper Bilodo could see his own face as though reflected by so many tiny mirrors, his anguish multiplied to infinity…

That's what he dreamt about, and when he woke, he really wasn't sure of anything any more, and was off for another ride on the rollercoaster of fear. He began to ponder if, rather than wait, he should perhaps take preventive action, if he shouldn't write Ségolène and own up to everything, let her know Grandpré was dead and he himself just a pathetic impersonator

– at least he'd be easing his conscience – but then he'd change his mind and tell himself to be reasonable again, knowing full well such a confession was impossible, it would have meant giving himself away and ringing the knell of the precious correspondence that was still, and now more than ever, the spice of his life.

Bilodo, as he veered back and forth like a weathercock between hope and resignation, could testify to it: there wasn't anything worse than waiting when you were unsure of the outcome.

* * *

Ségolène's reply finally came. Bilodo rushed out of his cubicle and barricaded himself in the men's toilets. He held his breath, preparing himself to find out what his audacity had cost him, and unfolded the sheet. A five-line poem. She replied with a tanka:

Steamy, sultry night
The moist sheets' soft embrace burns
my thighs and my lips
I search for you, lose my way
I am that open flower

Bilodo blinked, thinking he'd misread it, but no, he hadn't. There was no mistake. Those words were really the words, the lines really those lines, and the poem was *that* poem.

He had expected a disapproving letter, or perhaps a simple haiku of the kind they used to write to each other, or else, in the most favourable instance, a romantic tanka like his own, but surely not *this*, this surge of sensuality, this torrid poem. What had come over her? Bilodo felt a stirring in his pelvic region and realised he had an erection, an astonishing physiological occurrence that was all he needed to rattle him completely. Never had a letter from Ségolène provoked such a reaction. Not that it was the first time he had a hard-on in her honour, far from it – it happened all the time when he dreamt about her. But like this, in broad daylight, without the convenient excuse of being unconscious?

It was obviously due to the tanka's unusual content, its palpable eroticism. What he wished he knew was if Ségolène had foreseen the effect her poem might have. Was it accidental or deliberate? How was Bilodo supposed to respond? What could he possibly reply to something like *that*?

* * *

At night he dreamt about a snake slithering through ferns and crawling furtively among the smooth brown roots of a tree whose trunk was festooned with lianas. Except that the tree wasn't a tree but a body, the naked body of Ségolène asleep with her flute beside her. Quietly, so as not to waken her, the snake crept onto her throat, coiled around her limbs, slid between her breasts, slunk down onto her belly, tasted the air with its bifid tongue, then ventured even further down, towards that dark valley, that bushy triangle between her thighs… Bilodo, enthralled by the serpentine dream, woke up more excited than ever, although this had practically been his normal state since the previous day: his erection persisted, urgent, only vanishing briefly when he managed to put Ségolène's tanka out of his mind. As he reread the stanza, he wondered again if he perceived it correctly, if the sexual coloration he attributed to the poem wasn't a figment of his own depraved imagination, but came to the conclusion it wasn't. The tanka was raunchy, full stop. Whether Ségolène had meant it to be like this or had written it in all innocence, there was only one appropriate way to reply to it:

You are not just the flower
You're the whole garden
Your scents drive me wild
I enter your corolla
and I drink in your nectar

18

As the ocean licks the shore,
its surf a salty
kiss – so our lips lightly touch,
retreat, draw close again,
and lock at last

Chocolate Easter egg
trimmed with a yellow ribbon
The strap of your dress
has slipped down your bare shoulder
which I'd love to nibble on

Tender cannibal,
if you nibble me
you will have to eat me whole
or else you will be the one
who is gobbled up by me

I will be the wind
rippling through your hair
stealing its enticing scent
I will slip beneath your skirt
inflaming your skin

My toes are wriggling,
coiling and curling,
electrified with pleasure
It's because of my fingers
I think too hard about you

*   *   *

It was a sweet intoxication, a voluptuous fever that made you live life twice as intensely, a turbulent current you had no desire to struggle against, a current you could only surrender to, and besides, that was all Bilodo wanted. His only ambition was to continue the sensual adventure, the bold detailing of the body, and experience the ecstasy to the fullest. This pursuit occupied him completely. He hardly ever put his nose outside the door any more and remained indifferent to the loveliness of May, even though he liked that month better than any other. He hadn't gone back to the Madelinot; mortified that Tania could have thought he'd wanted to ridicule her, he daren't show his face there again. Actually, he no longer went to work. The opprobrium he was a victim of at the Depot had become unbearable to him, so he'd asked for and obtained a six-month unpaid leave. Now that his time was his own, he devoted himself entirely to Ségolène.

* * *

Your breasts on the horizon
a dune with satiny slopes
I long to taste their honey
to quench my thirst like
a vampire in love

Lost in the desert,
my thirsting mouth crawls along
At last the oasis, where
I dip the tip of my tongue
It is your navel

Your smooth, slender legs
catch the glow of a moonbeam
The sculptor who modelled them

availed himself of
the finest mahogany

Your hands lift me up
bend me, enfold me
fashion me, set me on fire
They do with me what they want
I'm a plaything in your hands

Under the screen of your dress
at the crossing of your thighs
a hidden river
secret Amazon
Let me make my way upstream

The cloth of your skin
sliding over mine
If only I could stitch them
together so they would touch
everywhere at the same time...

* * *

Was the tanka really the best tool when it came to chiselling desire? The form that had served Bilodo so well when it was a matter of putting feelings into words began to weigh him down, seemed too cerebral. Looking for a way to lighten his pen, he decided to go back to the basic simplicity of the haiku, more conducive, he felt, to the gushing forth of artesian urges.

Your breasts – twin mountains
Their proud erectile summits
rise up beneath my fingers

And Ségolène must have appreciated the initiative, since she lost no time in taking the same shortcut:

Robust root throbbing
in the palm of my hand,
gorged with burning sap

And so the history of the haiku's birth repeated itself: stripped of superfluous words as though they were clothes dropped on the way to the bedroom, the naked essence of the poetry emerged. But Bilodo wasn't satisfied: he couldn't take the slowness of regular post any more, so he switched to express post. Ségolène followed suit; thus the waiting period was shortened. The exchange sped up, breathing turned into panting, but it still wasn't fast enough for Bilodo, who began to post poems to the Guadeloupean woman without even waiting for her reply and was soon sending her a haiku a day. And Ségolène, too, began sending him haiku after haiku without bothering to wait for his. Almost every morning another letter from her fell on the doormat. The poems flew back and forth, fast and furious, without any chronological continuity now, yet still responding to one another in a peculiar way:

Flower of your flesh
Within its tender petals
lies a hidden pearl

Venture into the
Glowing warmth of me
Lash your body onto mine

I move towards you
Now you let me in
And all your mouths swallow me

You travel in me
you gaze upon my landscape
you swim in my lake

I travel in you
I reach the very centre
of your capital

Seaquake. I explode
deep inside of me
an inner supernova

Fiery tsunami
great surge of lava
I die everlastingly

Carried by the wave
I am nameless now
I am only a colour

Stars – shimmering spread of sails
the solar wind blows
to infinity

19

You can't have your head in the clouds forever. As gravity eventually caught up with Bilodo, he came back down to earth, still stunned by the slow explosion of the poetic orgasm he'd just experienced. It was true, then, that love gave you wings. Never before had he embraced a woman the way he just did in the heavenly spheres. He'd felt Ségolène so close, sensed her to be all his, totally within him as he'd been totally within her, and knew she, too, had undergone that inner explosion. He was sure she had come at the same time he had. What more could you write after that? What poem could you possibly compose that wouldn't disappoint after passion had been so completely satisfied? Something sweet whispered in the ear of the lover perhaps, before dropping off to sleep?

Searching for an idea, Bilodo put on his kimono, then glanced pensively at the window and saw scattered snowflakes drifting lazily down on rue des Hêtres. Winter already? Had *that* much time passed? Had summer shot by like a comet without him noticing, indifferent as he'd been to anything outside the boundaries of his inner world? Then, looking more closely, he realised it wasn't snow falling, but pollen raised by the wind, a spray of pollen coming from the trees in the nearby park. You couldn't tell the difference. Winter in the middle of summer. This surreal scene matched Bilodo's mood perfectly and gave him the inspiration for what to write:

Like a duvet on asphalt,
a shower of confetti,
the first snow softly
languidly settles
on your love-spent night body

* * *

Masquerade of clouds – the moon
slips into another skin
Tender this moment
on the veranda
when I think only of you

An arid canyon,
its rivers and creeks long gone,
where nothing will grow
Such is my desolate soul
between each of your letters

Day in and day out
wherever I am
you are always by my side
Before your poetry, I
didn't know I was alone

The dog is guarding
his sleeping mistress
He's ready to die for her
Allow me, Madam, poor fool
that I am, to be your knight

But you flatter me, dear Sir,
I am your humble servant
Still, should it strike your fancy,
I will also be
your Dulcinea

Windmills do not frighten me
nor do ferocious giants

All I fear is your
ennui when you see
my sorrowful countenance

*On the lycée wall
an ancient clock faithfully
gives the time to the
people in the neighbourhood
My heart beats for you alone*

* * *

Glancing by chance at a calendar, Bilodo was amazed to discover
that the month of August was already quite far advanced. It
would soon be a year since Grandpré had departed this world.
The fateful date that had heralded the dramatic change in
Bilodo's life was fast approaching, but he felt neither dread
nor sadness as the day drew near, because, much more than
a death, this anniversary would mark a birth, a rebirth – his own
– and the beginning of his tender correspondence with Ségolène.
Obviously, the event would only be significant for *him*: in *her*
eyes it would just be a day like any other, but even so the coming
to a close of this first year of bliss seemed worth commemo-
rating, if only in a discreet way:

I was bleak winter
then your poems were my spring,
your love the summer
What has autumn in store for
us with its russets, its gold?

Ségolène's reply, reaching Bilodo a few days later, plunged him
into a state of immeasurable horror.
Ségolène had high hopes for the autumn, too…

As a child I dreamt
of Canada's bright autumn
I have bought my ticket and
will arrive the twentieth
Will you have me, then?

20

The sweet, radiant dream of love was turning into a nightmare. Where did she get such a crazy notion? See the Canadian autumn? What was she driving at?

It was absolutely impossible. Ségolène couldn't show up in Montreal like that, or else it was all over, everything would crumble. How could the delusion continue, since she knew what Grandpré looked like, since there were those blasted photographs they'd exchanged? But how could he tell her not to undertake this insane trip? How was he to say no to her?

She would be coming on the twentieth of September, which gave Bilodo three weeks to find a suitable answer, to fabricate some sort of excuse. Perhaps he could write he'd had to go on a trip himself, that he had to be out of the country for all of September, so unfortunately he wouldn't be able to receive her. But what if she suggested putting off her visit to a later date, to after he got back?

* * *

How could she be so silly? Didn't she realise she would jeopardize everything, she was stupidly endangering the perfect relationship they'd had until then? But of course it wasn't her fault: she couldn't possibly know. Bilodo had to admit he was solely responsible for his misfortune. He should have had the good sense to anticipate what might happen, to guess it would come to this sooner or later. How could he have been so blind?

What to do? Inform her he'd recently undergone cosmetic surgery that had considerably altered his appearance? Or run away? Move immediately out of this apartment she knew the address of and where she'd inevitably turn up as soon as she arrived? Let her deal with the inexplicable mystery of his disappearance on her own? But how would he later be able to bear such a burden of guilt, of cowardice, of dashed hope? How could he forget, how could he survive?

* * *

There was no way out. Bilodo knew he was cornered, as hopelessly caught as an innocent mouse under the cruel steel of the trap. It was the end of the tranquil dream, the bursting of the happy bubble he'd been floating in for so long, and the rupture filled him with helpless anger. He couldn't resign himself to losing her but lacked the courage to face her. All the options were loathsome, all doors were closed. He had reached a terminal dead end.

* * *

It was early the next day when the phone rang. Not caring one way or the other, Bilodo let the answering machine kick in in the living room. Someone was leaving a message. It was a publisher, one of those he'd submitted the manuscript *Enso* to. The guy briefly explained he liked the collection very much, wanted to publish it, and asked that someone return his call without delay. Unfolding from the fetal position he'd been curled up in, Bilodo got up to go and listen to the message again. Fate sometimes had the oddest twists. This piece of news, which would have delighted him only a day earlier, now merely embittered him. What was the use? What difference could the publication of Grandpré's poems make in the impossibly tangled predicament he was in, except to complicate it even further? Wasn't the game up anyway?

Picking up the manuscript, he opened it at random, as you open a pack of tarot cards in search of a revelation, and came upon this haiku:

To break through the horizon
look behind the set
meet and embrace Death

The poem filled his soul, suddenly took on a new meaning, and Bilodo realised that was it: the only way out, the final solution to all his problems.

He straightened up. He knew what he had to do.

21

It was perfectly obvious. This was the course he needed to take, but not without first carrying out certain preparations. Bilodo wrote a note to that publisher who just called, giving him permission to publish *Enso* as he wished. He put the letter on the desk so it would easily be found, then gave Bill a double ration of his favourite yum-yums and said goodbye to the fish, thanking him for his unfailing friendship. He was now ready to go.

The large openwork beam adorning the living room ceiling would do very well. He pushed the little leaf-shaped table directly underneath, then removed the belt from his kimono and tested its strength. Satisfied, he reached into his childhood memories, going back to the carefree days when he belonged to the Cub Scouts, and effortlessly made a slip knot. He was bent on doing things neatly. There was no question of him slitting his wrists or using a gun, two equally disgusting methods. Bilodo wanted to depart this world with dignity, leaving a minimum of traces: hanging was no doubt the least messy way.

He climbed onto the little table, tied the end of the belt to the beam, then tightened the slip knot around his neck. He was ready. It was time to embrace Death. He only had to give a kick with his heel to tip the table and put an end to his suffering. Bilodo took a deep breath, closed his eyes and...

The doorbell pierced the silence.

Bilodo started, not sure what to do. He decided to wait a little while, hoping the intruder would go away, not ring again, but the doorbell sounded a second time. He experienced a peculiar mixture of relief and annoyance. Really! Who dared come and bother him at this crucial moment – he who hadn't had a visit from anyone in months? He removed the slip knot, stepped down from the table, went to the door, and peered through the spy hole. The distorted face that appeared on the other side belonged to Tania.

* * *

Tania. He had almost forgotten about her. If there was one last person to whom Bilodo still owed an explanation, it surely was the young waitress. With a vague feeling of dread, he unlocked the three locks, unlatched the four safety chains, and opened the door. As Tania caught sight of him in the doorway, she seemed even more startled than he was. She stared at him anxiously, asked if he was all right, and blurted out she found him greatly changed. This didn't surprise Bilodo: after so much turmoil, and the serious decision to embrace Death, he must have looked like someone who'd just returned from the grave. With the faintest of reassuring smiles he told her he'd never felt better. The young woman, who appeared unconvinced, apologised for bothering him, and explained in a muddled way she'd got his address through Robert. Bilodo wanted to apologise, too, for what happened at the Madelinot that last time, but she beat him to it, insisted a large part of the blame lay with *her*: having grilled Robert and got his confession, Tania knew Bilodo wasn't responsible for what had occurred and, besides, she felt it was mostly her own fault, since nothing would have happened if she hadn't indulged in imagining... things, wasn't that true?

She shifted from foot to foot, nervous, visibly embarrassed, looking as though she were waiting for him to confirm what she just said, or contradict it perhaps. Then, when nothing came, she went on to the other purpose of her visit and told him she was going away, she was moving, she was quitting her job at the restaurant to go and live in the suburbs.

Was she hoping for a particular reaction from him? Did his unresponsiveness disappoint her? If so, she didn't let on, but handed him a slip of paper and pointed out it contained her new address in case he... if ever he wanted to... well, anyway... As Bilodo examined the sheet, he noticed she'd taken the trouble to carefully calligraph her new address and phone number

Japanese-style, with a brush. The result looked quite lovely, and he complimented her warmly on it. She asked him to get in touch with her if ever it suited him. He promised he definitely would. He really shouldn't hesitate, she added further, forcing a smile. Then there was a brief, awkward silence. They just stood there, on the landing, not saying anything, afraid to look at each other, and this lasted a good ten, interminable, seconds. Finally Tania broke the stasis by telling him she had to go. She said goodbye and stiffly went down the steps.

On the pavement, she turned around to see if he was still there; then, quickening her pace, she hurried off. Bilodo thought he spotted something glistening on her cheek. A tear? When he saw her walk away, a powerful emotion swept over him. It was like a stinging void, like a beautiful thought that aborts just as it is about to take off, vanishing before it has even had a chance to take form. A sharp lump choked Bilodo's throat and he noticed his eyes were blurred with tears. He suddenly felt tempted to call Tania, to hail her before she was too far away, and his hand went up, stretched towards her, and he tried to shout, but no sounds escaped his lips. Once Tania reached the corner, she turned right and slipped out of sight. Bilodo's hand dropped.

On the street, the wind bit its tail, sending newspaper pieces swirling around and around. Bilodo looked up at the sky, saw it was overcast and grey, packed with heavy clouds. There was a storm in the air. He shivered, went back in.

* * *

Bilodo pensively closed the door and studied the sheet of paper with Tania's new address and phone number, no less fascinated by the beautifully calligraphed characters than by the new possibilities they suggested. The letters and figures seemed to float on the surface of the paper, to glow in the dusk. The great change the surprise visit had worked in him baffled Bilodo – that emotion the young woman's tear had stirred up, and that insane hope springing up all of a sudden just from the slip of paper she had left behind. Had he overlooked something terribly important, he wondered? Might there be a solution other than the ones he had considered until then, a better way to get out of the impasse he was in? Could there possibly be life after death or, better still, *before*?

He walked into the living room and froze, finding himself back in front of the slip knot hanging from the ceiling. He felt his stomach turn. The prospect of dying, which had seemed beneficial only a short while ago, now terrified him, and the thought of the act he had almost committed made him sick. Gripped by a violent wave of nausea, he ran to throw up in the bathroom.

When he finally stood up again, he felt literally drained and had to hold on to the sink so as not to collapse. He needed to freshen up. He ran the cold water, splashed his face numerous times. The wash made him feel a little better. He shook himself off, then cast a pessimistic glance in the mirror, just to see what zombie-like mug would be reflected there.

What he saw frightened him out of his wits. In the mirror loomed the bearded, dishevelled head of Gaston Grandpré.

22

Bilodo gazed in disbelief at the face that couldn't be there, that *shouldn't* be there in the mirror instead of his own because it belonged to a dead man. He tried to chase it away by blinking hard, then gave his head a stinging slap, but Grandpré remained stubbornly stuck in the glass, mimicking each of his gestures, watching him with a stupefaction no less than his own. Bilodo came to the obvious conclusion that he had gone mad. Soon after, certain facial details of the mirror's occupant aroused his attention and led him to reconsider this perhaps too-hasty judgement. It wasn't quite Grandpré. Those green eyes were Bilodo's, *not* the deceased's blue ones, as were those eyebrows – finer, less bushy than Grandpré's – and that slightly flat nose, and the much less fleshy bottom lip… As he slowly recognised himself deep within the other man's face, Bilodo acknowledged he wasn't dreaming, and hadn't slipped into psychosis, and that the guy opposite was really *him*, though altered in an almost unbelievable way.

Struggling to find a rational explanation, he understood that what he was observing in the glass was the result of a several months' lapse in personal hygiene. He had been so wrapped up in his poetic adventure that he'd completely forgotten to look after himself, neglecting the most basic body care, not even bothering to look at himself in the mirror, so that it had finally come to this: to this visual shock, this decadent image of himself. But – Bilodo wondered – could chance alone account for the extraordinary resemblance to Grandpré? Wasn't it due, rather, to an unconscious wish to identify with his predecessor? Perhaps Bilodo had been so eager to mistake himself for Grandpré he'd ended up looking like him to the point that one could be mistaken for the other. In any case, the illusion was startling: with his several months' growth of beard and his shaggy mane that hadn't seen a comb for just as long, and wrapped in Grandpré's kimono, he bore a striking resemblance to the deceased. No wonder Tania seemed so surprised when she caught sight of him looking like this: for a moment she must have thought she was seeing Grandpré's ghost.

Bilodo decided to tackle the thick beard covering his cheeks right away; he ran the hot water and got out his razor, but stopped in mid-gesture. An idea had just sprung into his mind: since Tania was fooled, even though she'd known the deceased well, and since Bilodo himself had been taken in for a short while, then why couldn't someone who'd only ever seen Grandpré in a photograph be fooled as well?

Transfigured, Bilodo put down his razor. The autumn rendezvous was suddenly becoming possible, wasn't it?

Why not seize this unique chance of welcoming Ségolène to his place? He longed to commune with her through the flesh as much as through words, didn't he? He yearned to love her in another way than in a dream, even though his body would take the place of Grandpré's, to truly love her as she deserved, as they both deserved, and finally start living for real.

Could he ignore such a wonderful opportunity to reverse fate? Did he even have the right?

So why was he still hesitating? What was keeping him from asking her to come and spend the autumn, the glorious Canadian autumn she had been dreaming about, in his company?

* * *

Fly to the autumn
It's waiting just for you to
display its brilliance

In his euphoria, Bilodo already pictured himself at the airport, welcoming the Guadeloupean woman as she timidly appeared at the arrivals gate, and imagined himself driving along with her through a magnificent, postcard autumn landscape, their hair streaming in the wind. Already he savoured their first kiss, anticipated the fiery first embrace, lost his way in Ségolène's morning hair spilled across the pillow. But for these wonderful visions to become reality, his haiku needed to be posted.

Bilodo had just put a stamp on the envelope when the sky rumbled outside. Thunder. Having threatened all morning, the storm was finally breaking; its first heavy drops crashed against the window glass in the living room. Bilodo refused to let the bad weather stop the poem being sent, so he grabbed an umbrella and went out. While he was still on the landing, a flash of lightning illuminated the street, followed instantly by a loud cracking noise, and suddenly the shower looked like a monsoon. On the other side of the street, through the sheet of rain, he glimpsed a postal van. Post collection time already? It must be, since Robert was there, in the downpour, hurriedly transferring the contents of the box to a sack. Bilodo hesitated. The clerk's presence bothered him. He hadn't spoken to Robert since the spring incidents and had no desire to be subjected to his taunts. Besides, Robert wasn't alone; there was a postman with him, most likely the one substituting for Bilodo in the area, a guy he didn't know, had never even seen, but whom he'd lately grown distrustful of, for he suspected him of trying to open some of Ségolène's letters.

The rain now came down in buckets. Robert, rushing to get out of the storm, closed the postbox again and chucked the sack into the van. He'd be leaving any minute now. Bilodo's wish to post the haiku prevailed over any other consideration: he resigned himself to swallowing his pride and let out a great shout to draw the clerk's attention. Robert turned around, spotted him. Brandishing his letter, Bilodo tore down the stairs and dashed out onto the flooded road. The other guy, the postman, started motioning with his arms, called out something indistinct to him. The blast of a horn pierced the air. Then there was a crash.

The world spun around Bilodo, in slow motion, as in a dream. He whirled around in space, wondering what was happening to him, then there was another crash, and the world became steady again, heavy, and hard beneath his back. The sky flashed and thundered, pelted his eyes with rain. He tried to move, but found he couldn't, and noticed he was in terrible pain. A figure placed itself between the storm and him. A familiar face, Robert's. Then another face appeared, the postman's, familiar too, but for a completely different reason: it was his own. The postman's face was that of the old Bilodo, Bilodo before the metamorphosis, the clean-shaven, clear-eyed Bilodo he had once been.

It was he himself, his former self, looking down at him from up there.

23

How could he find himself lying on the wet asphalt and be at the same time up there, watching himself? By what magic? Bilodo tried desperately to understand before it was too late, and the answer came to him, it seemed, through an inner voice whispering the words of the opening and closing haiku of Grandpré's collection:

Swirling like water
against rugged rocks,
time goes around and around

This was exactly what was happening. The past repeating itself. Time playing a nasty trick on him. As it swirled against the rock – set in the current – that was the moment of Grandpré's death-struggle, time had been caught in a kind of eddy, forming a loop trapping Bilodo.

Had Grandpré sensed this? As he wrote his haiku, had he known it was prophetic?

A life in the shape of a loop. Bilodo had run aground on the shoals of time. This was so unbelievably, so magnificently absurd that in spite of the excruciating pain he could only laugh about it. He laughed, swallowing rainwater, and the more he laughed, the funnier it all seemed to him. Then a lump came into his throat and his laughter ceased. There really wasn't anything amusing about it. In fact, it was tragic: he was dying after all, without any consolation, without the comfort even of knowing his death would be a release, because he only needed to look at the other Bilodo, look at the eager way he eyed the letter between his fingers, to understand that the film wouldn't end here, that his turn would come and the loop would continue, carrying him, too, to his death, and then the one who came after, and the one who followed him as well, and so on forever. It was as cruel as that: Bilodo was condemned to an endlessly recurring death, and nothing could ward off this curse. Except perhaps…

Holding the letter back… preventing it from slipping into the gutter… hanging on to it long enough for the other Bilodo to grab it, maybe read it, and perhaps decide to post it, thus steering his life into a different time stream… and then who knew? The loop might be undone and damnation averted. Mustering whatever strength he had left, he directed it towards the fingers of his right hand, which tightened on the letter. He closed his eyes the better to focus his willpower, and an unusual image appeared on the screen of his closed eyelids: a red circle or, rather, a revolving wheel of fire.

Still the cursed loop. The serpent bit its tail. Time cannibalized itself.

Suddenly, in Bilodo's mind, the memory resurfaced of those obscure syllables, those final words Grandpré had murmured just before he expired: 'in-sole', he thought he heard. He hadn't understood at the time what it was about, but now he knew with dazzling certainty.

'*Enso*,' he moaned as the last breath of life abandoned him.

Biographical notes

About the Author

Denis Thériault's first novel, *L'iguane* (*The Iguana*), was published to great critical acclaim and won three major literary prizes. His second novel, *Le facteur émotif* (*The Peculiar Life of a Lonely Postman*) won the Japan-Canada Literary Award in 2006. Born on the north shore of the Gulf of St Lawrence, near Sept-Îles, Quebec, Denis Thériault has a degree in psychology and is an award-winning screenwriter who lives with his family in Montreal. His work has been translated into many languages.

About the Translator

Liedewy Hawke has won the Canada Council Prize for Translation and the John Glassco Translation Prize. She has been nominated four times for the Governor General's Literary Award for Translation. She translates French-language as well as Dutch-language literary works. She lives in Toronto.

Q&A with the author

What inspired you to write *The Peculiar Life of a Lonely Postman*?

Often the inspiration for what I write comes from my dreams, but in this case it was different: the original idea for *The Peculiar Life of a Lonely Postman* came to me from a very concrete incident. A few years ago, while I was checking the day's post after the postman had been, I noticed an envelope whose corner seemed partially unsealed, as if somebody had tried to open it, and that was what started the creative process. I immediately imagined an indiscreet postman who kept certain personal letters for himself and brought them back home, steamed them open and read them with curiosity: Bilodo was born, and his story rapidly took form in my mind.

What made you choose to focus on Japanese culture and the art of haiku and tanka writing?

It was not there at first. This immersion in the universe of haiku and Japanese culture was not part of the original plan of the novel. It is a discovery that I made when the manuscript was already well advanced. In the first version, the letters from Ségolène that Bilodo intercepted were written in prose, but I was not satisfied with the effect it produced – I thought it was not special or 'magic' enough to really impassion Bilodo. I sought another solution, a better idea, and it is in a book of haiku, opened a little by chance, that I found it. I knew immediately that it was what I needed: haiku, these small moments of eternity in seventeen syllables, could really fascinate Bilodo to the point of falling in love with a woman that he did not know. I thus made the decision to rewrite the whole manuscript, integrating this new poetic dimension, and all the rest, the evocation of the Japanese culture and the focus on Zen philosophy, followed naturally, giving the novel a depth which was missing until then.

Are you a fan of poetry?

I like poetry but I am certainly not an expert. I know the French and Canadian classical poets quite well, but there are gigantic holes in my lyric culture. I write little poetry myself; perhaps I would never have thought of creating haiku if it had not proven to be essential for the writing of *The Peculiar Life of a Lonely Postman*. In fact, I learned how to write haiku specifically for this novel. One could say that I reproduced the behaviour of my hero Bilodo: I researched and read the Japanese masters, then I tried to write some haiku, and learned little by little. For approximately four months, I wrote nothing but haiku day after day, by the hundred, until I acquired a certain knowledge of this simple yet complex art. Then, I realised I had to face a second challenge: for the story to function well, Bilodo's first poetic attempts necessarily had to be awkward; we had to feel a progression in his apprenticeship of the art of haiku. After having learned how to write 'good' haiku, I needed to learn how to write some 'bad' ones, then 'less bad', and then 'not that bad', 'almost good', etc. It was a most instructive exercise, which I recommend without hesitation to anyone who nourishes poetic ambitions.

Would you describe the book as a love story, a tragedy or something else entirely?

It certainly is a love story, but also a psychological novel that flirts with the fantastic. In my view, it is an intimist tale on the themes of loneliness, dreams and imagination. It is the story of an overly curious postman whose love for an unknown woman leads him to question his own identity, and finally fall into some kind of cosmic trap... the nature of which we will not reveal out of respect for the future readers of the book.

**When creating the character of Bilodo did you intend
for readers to sympathise with or pity him?**

I was a little concerned about the way Bilodo would be perceived. I feared he would be found distant, antipathetic, seen perhaps as a sociopath. Personally, I feel quite close to him. In my view, Bilodo is an eminently modern character: he is isolated in his personal bubble, takes refuge in the small virtual universe, so comfortable, which he created for himself; in this twenty-first century, I believe that many of us resemble him. Bilodo fears peoples, and love frightens him – he prefers to live in the wonderful imaginary world that he has invented around Ségolène. He's a paradoxical being, pitiful and admirable at the same time. Bilodo is a dreamer, but an active one, a kind of poetic warrior who will fight until death to preserve his ideal.

**Did you know what the end of the book would be when
you started writing?**

Yes, but it was another ending, because the initial plan of the novel evolved during the process. As I explained previously, the idea of including haiku changed everything, and forced me to rewrite the novel from the beginning, to imagine a new ending. Which confirms this eternal truth, always new for me: when you write, the best part is never what you had planned but what you discover on your path.

How did you first get into writing?

I started very young. I learned to read before going to school, and soon became a voracious reader of anything that fell under my hand, including books that were quite ahead of my age and often beyond my comprehension. By eight or nine, I was writing little stories, little poems, and some short plays which I forced my friends to act out. I was very interested in theatre. I wanted to become an actor, a director, a playwright. So I studied theatre, and did all these things in my twenties. Then

I became a screenwriter, a profession that I still practise today. The idea of becoming a novelist came to me quite late, in my mid-thirties, when I realised that the ultimate freedom for a writer was to create novels. I could say that I came to it by process of elimination, after having turned my hand to many trades: it was in the end the only job that was really appropriate for me. And I know I will never stop doing that even if it drives me mad sometimes: a small price to pay for living in a passionate way.

How does it feel to have won three prestigious literary prizes? (The Prix Anne-Hébert, the Prix France-Québec/ Jean Hamelin, and the Prix Odyssée)
I won these three prizes for another novel which I wrote, entitled *The Iguana* (*L'iguane*). *With The Peculiar Life of a Lonely Postman*, I won the Canada-Japan Literary Prize. Winning a prize is a marvellous thing; it is like a gift offered by destiny. Personally, I do not see it as the crowning of a work but rather an encouragement to continue, to go further. And it is my sincere ambition to write better novels. Although I am currently finishing my fourth novel, I have the feeling that I have hardly begun my writing career. I have plans for writing projects for the rest of my days, and several future lives.

Do you have a writing routine?
I am a disciplined person, but I do not have an immutable routine. I work six to eight hours each day, but it could also be the middle of the night sometimes. I always put some music on, mostly films soundtracks because of the variety of emotions and dramatic climates which they induce. In the middle of the afternoon, I usually walk to a little restaurant near my office, where I have a coffee. And at night, after work, I like to prepare supper and drink a bottle of good wine with my wife.

How much are novel writing and screenwriting interchangeable for you?

These are very different writing techniques which are not interchangeable, but they can influence each other. Very consciously, I write my novels on the classical structure of a film. The screenwriter is never very far behind the novelist, but he stays in the shadow; it is necessary to make good literature. Writing for theatre, TV, film or a novel is always writing, but the technique differs very much, as to the point of view, I would say. The focus is not the same. When you write a play, essentially, you write dialogues, you tell the story of people who talk to each other. At the other end of the spectrum, there is cinema, which is a medium of image and sound; when you write for cinema, you must think in terms of images, music and action; dialogues are important but not essential – you could very well have a film without a single spoken word. Writing for TV falls somewhere between these two. But writing a novel is a different experience. I consider it 'total writing'. At the same time, you are the playwright, the actors, the director, the composer and the cameraman. And you must mix all these elements in a literary way, with a style that has to be yours and nobody else. For me, novel writing is the ultimate form of storytelling.

The book has been compared to Julian Barnes and Haruki Murakami, so how does this make you feel?

Flattered, of course, to find myself in such an excellent company. And slightly embarrassed too; I must confess I have never read yet anything from Murakami, whom I know only by reputation – a gap which I intend to fill very soon. I have the highest esteem for Julian Barnes, this Master of contemporary literature. I am not sure that my style resembles his, but I certainly feel some kind of philosophical bond with this exceptional author. The reasons which make us compare an author with another always seemed strange to me. In some cases, there is obviously a common inspiration, but sometimes it is purely instinctive: a detail, a sentence, a simple word, and an association is created. Anyway, I will take these comparisons like a compliment that is perhaps a little too flattering.

The book was originally published in 2008 by a Canadian publisher – how do you feel about it now getting a new life through UK publisher Hesperus Press and do you like the repackage and new title?

The market for Canadian books is quite limited because of the crushing presence of our gigantic American neighbour. I was happy to learn that the novel would be published in the UK by Hesperus Press, and could thus join more readers. And I am delighted that we decided to keep the excellent English translation of Liedewij Hawke, a woman of talent, and also a friend. I do not want to compare the two books, but the new Hesperus version looks very attractive to me: the book is beautiful. If I were not the author, I would desire very much to read it.

Which other writers inspire you?

Hergé, Homer, Jules Verne, Edgar Poe, Maupassant, G.G. Marquez, Kafka, Boris Vian, François Villon. If I was asked to choose my favourite novel or work of fiction of all times, I would hesitate between *Perfume* (Süskind), *Alice in Wonderland* (Lewis Carroll), *Malpertuis* (Jean Ray), and *Les chants de Maldoror* (Lautréamont).

The book is very cinematic, in your mind, who would play Bilodo and Ségolène in the film?

While I wrote the novel, I imagined Bilodo as a young Adrian Brody, and Ségolène as a young Halle Berry. Of course, these excellent actors aren't appropriate ages for the roles. It would be necessary to choose actors of the same 'type' in a younger generation.

Are you working on anything new at the moment?

I am currently finishing a new manuscript. It is a novel which I started to write last year, not knowing at that point that *The Peculiar Life of a Lonely Postman* would be published at Hesperus Press: in fact, it is volume two of this story. It is the continuation of Bilodo's adventures, and more precisely those of Tania, the young waitress from the restaurant Madelinot in the first novel, who secretly loves our postman... Please, permit me to stay discreet about this for now.

Reading Group Discussion Questions

- Do you feel sympathy for Bilodo?
- In our modern world of social media do you think the art of letter writing is dead?
- How did reading the haiku and tanka add to your reading experience?
- Did you know much about haiku writing before reading the book and how do you feel afterwards?
- What moments did you find humorous and why?
- Is this a love story?
- Why do you think Bilodo was so isolated?
- Do you think true love can thrive after deception?
- How do you think the situation would have played out had Ségolène actually gone to Canada?
- Do you think it is possible to fall in love with someone you haven't met before?
- What do you make of the theory of Enso?
- What do you think Bilodo found so attractive about Japanese culture?
- Did you find Bilodo's actions plausible?
- Did you see the ending coming?

The Merman
by Carl-Johan Vallgren

Nella and her brother Robert live a difficult life with their mother and father in a small town on the west coast of Sweden. Robert is bullied at school, and Nella has to resort to debt and petty crime to pay off his tormentors.

When she turns to her friend Tommy for help, her suspicions are aroused by the mysterious comings and goings of his brothers at their dilapidated boat house. But when she uncovers the reason behind their enigmatic behaviour, her life is opened to the realities of a mindboggling secret.

The Merman is an exhilarating and beautiful book about sibling love and betrayal – and what happens when the mundane collides with the strange and wonderful.

'An intense little gem' *Dagens Nyheter*, Sweden

'Worthy of Stephen King on a good day' *Expressen*, Sweden

'Bitterly harsh and beautiful' *Svenska Dagbladet*, Sweden

PRAISE FOR CARL-JOHAN VALLGREN:

'Charged, atmospheric, thought-provoking' *Daily Telegraph*

'Challenging and shocking' *The Guardian*

NOW AVAILABLE

The Best Book in the World
by Peter Stjernström

Two authors. One idea. Who will be the first to write the best book in the world?

Titus Jensen is waiting for his big break. But he's middle-aged, has a fondness for alcohol and never gets taken seriously.

Eddie X is cool. Eddie X is a hit with the ladies and loves being the centre of attention. A radical poet and regular on the festival circuit, he is looking for his next big project to gain more adoring fans.

One night, after a successful literary event at which Titus reads from *The Diseases of Swedish Monarchs* and Eddie X waxes lyrical to the thrashing tones of metal band The Tourettes, the unlikely pair get horribly drunk together and hatch a plan. There's only one thing for a budding writer to do to get worldwide recognition: write the best book in the world – a book so amazing that it will end up on all the bestseller lists in every category imaginable, thriller, self-help, cookery, business, dieting… a book that combines everything in one!

But there is only room for one such amazing book and as the alcohol-induced haze clears Titus and Eddie X both realise they are not willing to share the limelight. Who will win the race to write the best book in the world, and to what unimaginable lengths will they go to get there first…?

'Well written and enjoyable' *Aftonbladbet*

'Spot on satire' *Stockholms Fria Tidning*

'Funny, original and lovingly disrespectful' *Tidningen Kulturen*

NOW AVAILABLE

The Hundred-Year-Old-Man Who Climbed out of the Window and Disappeared

by Jonas Jonasson

Sitting quietly in his room in an old people's home, Allan Karlsson is waiting for a party he doesn't want to begin. His one-hundredth birthday party to be precise. The Mayor will be there. The press will be there. But, as it turns out, Allan will not…

Escaping (in his slippers) through his bedroom window, into the flowerbed, Allan makes his getaway. And so begins his picaresque and unlikely journey involving criminals, several murders, a suitcase full of cash, and incompetent police. As his escapades unfold, Allan's earlier life is revealed. A life in which – remarkably – he played a key role behind the scenes in some of the momentous events of the twentieth century.

'Arguably the biggest word-of-mouth
literary sensation of the decade'
The Independent

'Imaginative, laugh-out-loud bestseller'
Daily Telegraph

'Should carry a health warning for spouses or partners who are easily irritated by the sounds of helpless chortling'
The Irish Times

NOW AVAILABLE

Wakolda
by Lucía Puenzo

José is hiding a terrifying secret. A seemingly charming doctor, behind his cool exterior lies a calculating, sadistic character.

On the run from his native Germany, José finds himself in South America where he plans to continue with his secret genetic experimentation. But his vision is put on hold when he meets Lilith in a small, run-down village. Although vivacious and beautifully blonde, she has a growth defect and, for José, represents all that he would like to exterminate from humankind. An anomaly amongst her perfect Aryan siblings, Lilith's existence intrigues him, and when he discovers that her mother is pregnant again, potentially with twins, the temptation to meddle in their lives and test his medical theories is strong.

Dark times lie ahead for Lilith and with few places to turn to for comfort, she clings ever tighter to her mysterious doll Wakolda.

And so begins a dark relationship between the doctor and little girl, the kind of love that simply cannot end well – for José is concealing the fact that he is the Nazi doctor Josef Mengele, infamous for performing experiments on humans at Auschwitz. And sooner or later his past is going to catch up with him.

NOW AVAILABLE

Under our three imprints, Hesperus Press publishes over 300 books by many of the greatest figures in worldwide literary history, as well as contemporary and debut authors well worth discovering.

Hesperus Classics handpicks the best of worldwide and translated literature, introducing forgotten and neglected books to new generations.

Hesperus Nova showcases quality contemporary fiction and non-fiction designed to entertain and inspire.

Hesperus Minor rediscovers well-loved children's books from the past – these are books which will bring back fond memories for adults, which they will want to share with their children and loved ones.

To find out more visit www.hesperuspress.com
@HesperusPress